DEAD & GONE

GRAVE TALKER SERIES BOOK TWO

ANNIE ANDERSON

DEAD AND GONE

Grave Talker Book 2

International Bestselling Author
Annie Anderson

Edited by Angela Sanders
Cover Design by Tattered Quill Designs

www.annieande.com

For those that have no idea what potential they possess.
It's way more than you think.

GRAVE TALKER SERIES

Dead to Me

Dead & Gone

Dead Calm

SOUL READER SERIES

Night Watch

Death Watch

ROGUE ETHEREAL SERIES

Woman of Blood & Bone

Daughter of Souls & Silence

Lady of Madness & Moonlight

Sister of Embers & Echoes

Priestess of Storms & Stone

Queen of Fate & Fire

PHOENIX RISING SERIES

(Formerly the Ashes to Ashes Series)

Flame Kissed

"In one aspect, yes, I believe in ghosts, but we create them. We haunt ourselves."

— LAURIE HALSE ANDERSON

"Take care of yourself, kid. And stay out of trouble," Siobhan instructed as she handed me my belongings in a giant Zip-Lock bag, along with a clipboard for me to sign. The exit from lock-up was not unfamiliar to me, but I'd never been on the receiving end of this little song and dance.

"Oh, you know me," I answered noncommittally. I had precisely zero intention of staying out of trouble. In fact, I was actively planning on getting into a whole heap of it the first chance I got.

"Yeah," she barked, her voice like stone, "I do." She knocked a dark braid off her shoulder, staring me down. No one could get anything past her, and it would be foolish to try.

Siobhan Byrne was an intuitive or possibly a psychic

of some sort. She couldn't see things clearly, but she just *knew* stuff. It made her a force to be reckoned with in a place like this—especially when rivaling factions started to get restless. The Arcane Detention Center was just like any other jail I'd ever been to. That was, if you took away the guards with magic, and the runes carved into every surface to dampen the prisoners' abilities, then sure, it was totally the same.

Siobhan was always in the right place at the right time, squashing brawls before they turned into full-blown riots. But she didn't know everything, and I'd saved her ass in the cafeteria one day early in my stay. We'd become fast friends, and I'd kept my eye out for her as much as I could for someone on the wrong side of the bars.

Compared to the other inmates, my stay at this facility had been relatively short. Still, nine months in lock-up was a long time to wonder if my life would ever be normal again. Add in my daily visits from a team of Arcane Bureau of Investigation nerds who were trying to figure out the limits of my abilities, and the better part of a year seemed to stretch on forever.

"I told you to stay out of trouble, and that is what you'll do, Darby," Siobhan ordered, and I fought the urge to snap-to and salute her. "You know good and well they're watching you."

By "they," she meant the ABI, but I wasn't stupid. If they could have implanted a Lo-Jack in my ass, they would have. I had zero doubts I didn't already have a magical equivalent on me somewhere.

I stared up into her bright-green eyes—and I do mean up. Siobhan had to be six and a half feet tall and was built like a feminine linebacker. She was what I would assume Valkyries looked like. Her dark hair was an impressive assortment of braids and dreads, with gold wire weaved into a few. Cuffs and rings adorned others. I could easily envision her in combat leathers and face paint, fighting off the British.

"I'm aware," I muttered, grumpily scratching my signature on the form. After getting out of here, my first order of business was figuring out how to punch Mariana Adler right in the face.

After that, I, of course, wanted world peace.

Siobhan snorted like she could read my mind. "Fair enough. Don't forget to say hi to that big hunk of man-meat waiting for you out there."

She skirted the tall desk and wrapped me in a bone-crushing hug. I could only assume she meant my partner, Jeremiah, but I couldn't for the life of me figure out why he would be waiting for me. As far as I knew, J had no idea I had been sent to ABI prison. Hell, before nine this morning, even I hadn't known I was going to be given my walking papers.

"And don't worry, your house has been taken care of while you've been away. Your pops is a sweetheart. I bet even your kitchen is clean as a pin. Give him a big hug when you see him, will you?"

As happy as I was to not be going home to a rancid fridge and a house left sitting for almost a year, just thinking about my dad made my heart hurt. I'd dreamt about him—and the act that got me shoved in here—every single minute I'd been stuck in this place. Would I hug him? Probably. Would I also sock him in the gut? That was also on the table. But I didn't say any of that out loud.

"Will do. Stay safe in here, will ya?" I muttered before letting her go.

As sad as I was to leave Siobhan to this place, I wasn't too eager to stay. I missed my life. I missed my house and my bed. But most of all?

I missed coffee.

Fun fact: I hadn't realized when I'd agreed to this deal that I would have to go without the good stuff. Especially not for this long. What kind of evil being decided this as a punishment?

I'd been poked, prodded, evaluated, and studied like a lab rat. That, I was all fine with. But no coffee?

Yeah... Fuck Mariana Adler and the horse she rode in on.

My first step into the Tennessee spring air was bittersweet. For the last nine months, the near-constant buzz of souls and ghosts I'd lived with the majority of my life had been muted. I couldn't see the specters, but I'd known they were there. While I seriously doubted there were no ghosts within those walls, I hadn't been able to see their nearly see-through forms.

The whispers had been dulled, the buzz muted. Even with every single bit of juice I'd absorbed, my abilities in that place had been damn near null.

I'd figured out pretty quickly that the warding etched into every single surface made it impossible for me to see much of anything. The scientists had taken a while to come to that conclusion themselves, and their testing ramped down to only clinical study. I couldn't say how many biopsies, vials of blood, and scans they'd done, but I knew if I never saw another needle in my life, it would be too soon.

As soon as I crossed the threshold to the outside world, the noise came rushing back. I hadn't realized just how loud it had been, how much I'd ignored it over the years. How much I had inured myself to the knowledge that death clung to my very mind. Or maybe since I'd finally come into my real self, the call of the souls had grown even louder now.

Last year, I'd just been trying to get by—trying to keep my little "seeing dead people" secret from the humans in my midst, trying really hard not to go crazy, and most of all, trying to do my job.

Somehow, I'd mostly managed all three. Except for being a certified ABI criminal, everything was turning up aces.

With the gray building at my back, I walked further into the sun. The buzz in my head that told me when specters were near reached a crescendo. The signature was familiar, but I couldn't say I was particularly thrilled to feel it again.

Hildenbrand O'Shea had been haunting me since I was a kid, the puberty bitch-slap turning my abilities to eleven. One second I'd been a normal kid, and the next, I was a ghost-seeing freak. Only recently did I find out Hildy was actually my grandfather. Given that he'd died sometime in the 1840s, it shattered the idea that my mother was anything close to human.

Hildy had kept a hell of a lot from me in the decade and a half he'd been in my life. I wasn't just going to sweep that shit under the rug on the bullshit basis of family. Especially with how much his silence had cost me.

"Lass," Hildy crooned, his Irish lilt grating my nerves. I hadn't spoken to him since the debacle at Whisper Lake.

That little croon made me want to smash shit. It made me want to see if the juice I'd absorbed still lingered in my tissues.

"You don't get to call me that," I growled through gritted teeth. "You don't get to play the wounded party. You don't get to come to me like your actions didn't set into motion the worst moment of my life. You don't get to play buddy-buddy when you sat on not only my abilities, but my lineage for damn near two decades."

I was leaving shit out. Hell, I was leaving out the mother of all things, but I hadn't entirely processed that bomb yet.

Later. Processing could be done much later.

"You don't," I whispered, "get to pretend you didn't do me wrong, Hildenbrand." I turned my head to look at him then, his gray form a washed-out version of who he'd been in life. Hildenbrand O'Shea had been a renowned grave talker, his name living on in infamy, even after his death nearly two centuries ago. Blond-haired and blue-eyed, I resembled him a bit. Turn me into a dude and give me a top hat and cane, and we could practically be twinsies.

It was tough realizing that I'd gotten so many things

from a man I despised.

"*Lass*," he implored, but I'd already had enough. His silence had made me watch my father die in my arms. His silence made it so I had to strike a deal I didn't want to make with a woman I would love to light on fire.

My left palm lit up for a single second, the remnants of a power I still didn't understand lingering under my skin. No way was I wasting it. Before Hildy could say another word, I balled my hand into a fist and socked him right in his stupid, spectral nose. His ghostly body went flying, and I watched with no small amount of satisfaction as he landed with a ghostly thud on the steps of the ghastly ABI detention center.

Shock colored his face as he wiped a glowing spectral ribbon of blood from his nose.

"You are not welcome in my home," I growled, my voice laced in a powerful command I had never used on Hildy. Not ever. "You are not welcome in my life. Why don't you go bother your daughter? You two liars deserve each other."

There had been no good reason for Hildy's betrayal, and all his posturing that he'd been doing it for my own good, was a whole load of bullshit I refused to swallow.

Hildy's face turned resolute, and he winked out of sight, leaving me to go fuck off somewhere else.

Good.

"Out less than a minute and already talking to spirits and punching ghosts. Way to go, Adler."

That smooth voice did not belong to my best friend, J. Oh, no. I wasn't that lucky. The big hunk of man-meat Siobhan had been talking about was not my partner, but the death mage ABI agent who'd simultaneously saved my bacon and torched it.

I swung my head to face Bishop La Roux, straightening my shoulders like I was going to have to punch him, too.

Dressed in a criminally hot pair of jeans and a T-shirt that should be illegal in at least five states, Bishop held out a bag with a very familiar logo on it like he was warding off a lion. Ignoring his messy hair and scruffy beard, I met his coal-dark eyes with suspicion. But instead of punching him like I had Hildy, I snatched the *Si Señor* bag from his hands, opened it, and dug in. The prison fare was a step above cat food, in my opinion, and just the thought of that yummy bit of heaven made my mouth water.

"Good to see tacos still work," he said, chuckling. "You need a ride home?"

The last time he'd needed to bribe me, he'd done it with these tacos. Good god in heaven, I was a pushover. I ignored the ridiculously hot man in favor of unwrapping a taco one-handed and shoving an end in my mouth. My teeth crunched into the blissfully crispy half-steak, half-pork taco, and my eyes rolled back in my head.

I had vastly overestimated prison food. This was the best thing I had *ever* eaten, and not a single soul on this planet could tell me any different.

"Maybe," I said around a mouthful of food. If he were any other man, I *might* have felt weird about my rudeness, but just like Hildy, Bishop was on thin ice. Though, tacos were an excellent way to strengthen his footing.

That taco was gone in another two bites, and I swallowed the yumminess before continuing, "How'd you hear about me getting out? Even I didn't know until today."

Bishop gave me a sly smile. "A little birdy told me."

I nodded, the answer dawning on me. "How is Sarina these days?"

Sarina Kenzari was Bishop's partner and a certified psychic and telepath. She called herself an oracle, but psychic was just as good a word as any. Out of everyone, she had been the only one to level with me about what she could and *could not* say. Though, Sarina couldn't "see" me like she could others. To her, I was a big, old blurry spot.

"She's good. She says hi. So, how about that ride?"

I let my gaze stray to the barren parking lot in front of the building. A lone, shiny black truck parked near the street broke up the desolate landscape of naked trees and cracked asphalt. A small cluster of staff vehicles were situated at the far end of the lot. I took a gander behind me to see if the building matched the unfortunate parking lot. I'd been blindfolded when Mariana brought me here nearly a year ago, and it was exactly what I would expect a haunted asylum to look like, even though I knew it had to be a glamour.

Nothing says "stay the fuck away" like the threat of a good haunting.

"I suppose you could give me a ride if you don't have anything better to do," I conceded, my tone only mildly petulant.

I had to wonder how in the hell I was supposed to make it out of here if Bishop hadn't been nice enough to pick me up. I hadn't been allowed calls or emails, which I thought was bullshit. Even regular inmates got some form of contact.

But not me.

"No, Adler," Bishop said, his voice a hell of a lot closer than it had been a few seconds ago. I whipped my head back to find him solidly in my space. "I don't have anywhere else I want to be."

Well, okay then.

2

The last time Bishop had been in my space like this, I'd threatened to unman him in the middle of the homicide bullpen. Now, not so much.

Heat hit my cheeks as I skirted around him, heading for the big black truck. The agent seemed so proper, I'd thought he'd be in a sedan or cop car. This seemed so... down-to-earth, a term I'd never peg for Bishop.

The deal I'd struck with my—*Mariana*—had been three-fold. The first condition was that my father be left alive. After all I had done to bring him back after Tabitha, it was only fair. The second was that J be left alone. My best friend and partner had only done what he had to, to keep me safe. As a human, he'd had no call to be anywhere near our arcane dealings.

But the third condition was probably the biggest ask of all the things I'd demanded. In exchange for my compliance with my punishment, I demanded Bishop not be disciplined for saving my father. Sure, Killian Adler was not my biological father. Still, he'd been my only family after my mother abandoned me under the guise of her faked death. And even though I kinda wanted to punch him in the face, too, I still loved him more than anything.

As far as I was concerned, Bishop and I were square. Though, I had a feeling he had other ideas.

Bishop relieved me of my giant Zip-Lock. The contents were likely just my bloody clothes and hopefully a cellphone and the keys to my house. Overtaking me to beat me to the passenger door, he opened it with a gallant flourish.

It had been a while since anyone had opened my door for me other than J. J was a good old Southern boy who'd been conditioned by his mama. Bishop was a whole different animal.

"Don't look so stunned, Darby. You'll start catching flies."

Snapping my mouth shut, I slid into the truck. I wasn't a short woman, but I still needed to do a little hop to seat myself. Inside, the vehicle smelled like rich leather and brand-new car. If the thing had just fallen off the assembly line, I wouldn't have been surprised. There wasn't a speck of dust on the dash, not an errant crumb in the cupholder. I kept my Jeep clean, but this was *clean*.

Bishop rounded the truck and took the driver's seat, and it reminded me of the last time I'd been in a car with him. He'd taken care of me when I'd been exhausted and scared, got me food, and drove me home. I still wondered if he'd done it to keep an eye on me or if it was something else.

Likely feeling my stare, he met my gaze. "What?"

I couldn't help it; I asked the question I'd been dying to ask him since I heard his voice. "Why are you here? Why out of everyone are you the one to pick me up?"

Something akin to shame crossed his expression. "I know what you did. I know, Darby. You saved my ass. You... I just know what you sacrificed, okay?"

I wondered if Sarina told him or if it was someone else.

Did it matter? No.

Would I rather him not know? Absolutely.

Bishop knowing about the deal wasn't horrible or anything, it just made me feel weird and awkward and stupid. And desperate.

The man brought your father back from the dead, even though it was a potential death sentence. Get over your awkward, Darby.

My inner voice was dealing in hard truths today.

I shrugged. "It just means we're square. You saved my dad. I saved your bacon. Even-Steven."

Bishop leaned over the center console, getting right in my space as much as the truck would allow. "We are not square, Adler, and you know it. I owe you."

This felt like flirting, but I was way too frazzled to do anything about it. The best I could do—because I was a socially inept nerd who hadn't had a date since the dawn of fucking time—was shrug.

Why, oh, why could I face him down when he was an asshole, but when he was nice, I got all… weird?

I began digging in the *Si Señor* bag for more goodies. "I shall take my payment in food, thank you."

Someone shoot me, please.

But my mouth would not let a question go unasked. "Were you flirting with me just then? I'm merely asking for educational purposes, so if you weren't, that is totally fine."

Bishop let out a bark of laughter, tossing his head back in a supremely sexy way as his whole body shook. Wiping tears of mirth from his eyes, he started the truck and put it in gear. "Yes, Adler, that was flirting. How long has it been since you had a date?"

I didn't even have to think about it. "College. I dated a guy for about a month before things got weird. When you talk to ghosts all the time, it's tough to keep a relationship. Either you know shit you aren't supposed to know, which makes you look like a stalker, or they think you're cheating on them because you look like you're talking on the phone to randos all the time. It was fucking exhausting, so I quit. Plus, Haunted Peak isn't exactly a hotbed of male prospects. Either they think I'm the town weirdo, have a creepy cop fetish and want me to handcuff them, or they think I'm batting for the other team. Plus, there is also a whole subset of misogynistic assholes who think that I shouldn't be a cop at all."

"Wait, wait, wait," he said while wiping at the air like he was trying to wash my words away. "Back up. You haven't dated anyone since college?" His voice even turned up at the end, almost in a squeak.

I bit into my taco while belatedly putting on my seatbelt. "Pretty much. I'm literally never alone, Bishop. Ne-ver. It's too exhausting to hide it all the time. You try dating a guy while his Aunt Mildred keeps shooting disapproving looks at you. Why do you think I have the best closed-case record in the county? It isn't because I have a personal life."

The only person with a record as clean as mine was J, and that was because he didn't date too much, either. It wasn't like he was in the closet or anything. J was just the pickiest man on the planet. I really needed to set him and Jimmy up.

"Okay." Bishop nodded thoughtfully. "How come you haven't dated any arcaners, then? You wouldn't have to hide from them."

How would I explain it? "Real talk? I haven't dated in so long, I wouldn't know where to start. I don't know how to flirt, and I'm pretty sure I've forgotten how to kiss."

Amongst other things.

"So if an arcaner who was super into you wanted to ask you out on a date, you would say…"

My lips pulled up into a grin all on their own. "Are you asking me on a date? Because that would affect my answer."

Bishop rolled to a stop at a light and shot me a look. "Doesn't know how to flirt my ass. Yes, I'm the one asking in this hypothetical scenario. What would you say then?"

I pretended to think about it, tapping my bottom lip with my finger for effect. "Will there be food on this date?"

The side of Bishop's mouth curled up. "Of course. Can't have you cranky."

"Then, sure," I chirped, shrugging like it was no big

deal. My squirmy insides would beg to differ, but he didn't need to know that.

"That's it? All I have to do is promise you food, and I'm in? Some standards, Adler."

It was my turn to laugh. "If you want me to, I can put you through the wringer. I figured we had enough history, you probably aren't a serial killer or a terrorist. Though, it's not like I can do a background check on you, now can I?"

"Not exactly. But Sarina would tell you all you wanted to know. There isn't a search database alive that can hold a candle to her."

"Then I guess I don't have anything to worry about."

Bishop muttered under his breath as he shook his head. I munched on tacos and fought off a smile. It had been a very long time since I'd flirted with anyone. Warmth suffused me as I kept right on eating. I couldn't remember the last time I'd had this much joy, this much relief. Usually, there was Hildy hanging around or a case to solve. There was a ghost to ignore or a whisper to pretend I wasn't hearing.

It felt strangely reminiscent of my childhood before my abilities came. If it weren't for the faint buzzing of Bishop's soul reminding me he was alive and would be for a very long time, I could almost forget the last nine months. I could forget the needle sticks and biopsies.

For a few minutes, I could almost believe the tests and prodding, and questions were just a horrible dream.

It wasn't long until we were back in Haunted Peak. My hometown was less town and more a small city. With over a hundred thousand people, it seemed to butt against the neighboring Knoxville more and more each year. It wasn't hard to miss the place, either. I'd lived here my whole life.

A life I'd thought was as happy as it could have been, given my penchant for talking to dead people. A small trill of anxiety filled me the closer we got to my house. I hadn't spoken to J or my dad or anyone in nearly a year. I hadn't gone a day without talking to either of them in longer than I could remember. Even though I was still pissed at my dad, I didn't want J thinking I'd abandoned him.

We'd had our ups and downs, but J had been the first person I'd told about Hildy and my odd little abilities. And if he didn't think I ghosted him, I wondered what he'd say about my actions up at Whisper Lake. It wasn't every day you saw your best friend stop an unhinged sorceress from raising a fucking deity.

Shuddering, I tried to wipe that entire experience from my brain. If I could have bleached it, I would have. A part of me wondered about my safety this close to the mountain. Knowing what was buried there, I contemplated whether or not Haunted Peak was the right place for me at all. But the other piece of my soul longed for my bed and my shower. Wanted the peace my home provided.

A peace that was instantly shattered when I spotted an unfamiliar car parked in my driveway.

"You know that car?" Bishop asked, his voice pitched low like someone could be listening as he pulled in behind the car, blocking it in.

When I shook my head, he bent to his ankle to draw his backup weapon. Handing it to me, I checked the mag and chambered a round. He killed his truck, and the pair of us got out at the same time. Bishop signaled that he would go around back, but I snagged a hand on his shirt.

With some back and forth—mostly in a truncated sort of sign language that barely gave each other the gist —he came around to my way of thinking. I gave him the nod, and his hands lit up with black and purple swirls of magic. With a flick of his fingers, my door flew open, revealing a pantsuit-clad woman in my favorite chair.

A woman I'd hoped to avoid for the rest of forever if I was lucky.

Mariana Adler.

3

My mother's blonde hair was coiffed in Hollywood-style glam waves, pairing perfectly with her red-painted lips. Her crisp suit and high heels and laissez faire attitude made me want to smash something. Add that to our strained relationship, and I had a hell of a time lowering my weapon.

Would the world miss a conniving grave talker with a penchant for keeping or spilling life-altering secrets at her mercurial whims? Likely not.

Mariana stared at my raised weapon with an unimpressed raised eyebrow, kind of like a mother would look at a tantrum-throwing toddler.

Fine, then.

I rolled my eyes and cleared the weapon before

handing it back to Bishop. I didn't need it anyway, and she knew it. "You're not welcome here. How about you do me an epic favor, and get the fuck out?"

It was bad enough she abandoned me and my father. Showing up here uninvited was just salt in the wound.

Mariana's smile was slow and bitchy. "Is that any way to talk to your mother?"

I couldn't help it, I gave her an indelicate scoff, the following laugh unbearably bitter. "My mother's dead. She died when I was nine. My father and I buried her. You're just some bitch wearing her face. Now get the fuck out of my house. You. Are not. Welcome here."

Mariana uncrossed and recrossed her legs, settling in for the long haul, and I had the urge to snatch Bishop's gun back and shoot her in the kneecap.

She'd heal. *Probably.*

"Don't you want to know why I'm here?" she asked, and I was reminded of Bishop sitting in that same chair asking me that same question. I had to wonder if that move was standard ABI protocol.

"I really don't. And I'll tell you just like I told Hildy. I don't want to talk to you. I don't want to see you. I don't want to know you. You are not welcome in my space. Now, I can exert some influence on Hildy because he's no longer alive. Would you like to join him?"

Mariana threw her head back and laughed.

She. Fucking. Laughed.

While sitting in my house, in my chair, knowing who my real father was and the power that was still thrumming in my veins. I didn't even get a chance to think about it before my feet carried me across the room and I was all the way in her space. Leaning over her in the chair, I put my face three inches from hers.

"Laugh again. I fucking dare you."

Mariana broke her gaze from mine to stare at my arms which were lit up like a damn Christmas tree. Her eyes traveled down my arms to my hands, which were gripping the chair and in serious danger of ripping it apart.

"Still juiced up, I see." Mariana's smile was snide, the arrogant twist to her lips practically begging me to slap the shit out of her. "I wonder what would happen if you got this angry at a human."

That doused my anger in a big, cold rush.

"Would they see you light up like a glowworm, exposing your secret and the existence of the arcane? Hmmm…" She seemed to ponder this thought, tapping her lip with a bright-red fingertip.

I straightened, taking three steps back as her intent became clear.

I'd just failed a test.

A big one.

"Well, since I don't think suspects are ready and willing to break into a cop's house, and I seriously doubt any of them betrayed me by faking their own death, I feel pretty confident it won't be an issue."

Mariana glanced past me and leveled Bishop with a skewering expression. "Have you seen her use her abilities in a public setting since her release?"

Oh, shit. Shitshitshit.

He totally had. I'd lit up like a glowstick when I punched Hildy in the face. And Bishop saw.

Fuuuuccccccckkkkkkk.

"No, Director, not that I saw," Bishop rumbled, lying through his fucking teeth like a pro. "Although we discussed difficult topics, Adler has displayed remarkable restraint."

Did she send him?

I didn't want the thought to cross my brain, but it did. I'd assumed it was Sarina who'd told Bishop about my release, but it just as easily could have been my mother. He'd never said one way or the other who had sent him to pick me up.

It was as if I'd been kicked in the gut. Even though he'd just lied to her for me, it felt wrong. All of this felt wrong.

"Very good. You are dismissed, Agent La Roux. Report to Agent Kenzari to receive your next assignment," Mariana said, shooing Bishop out of my house like she had the right.

"Excuse me," I practically shouted, ready to rip her in half, but Bishop stopped me.

"No, she's right," he murmured, putting a calming hand on my arm. "I need to get back. Good to see you again, Adler." He gave my mother a deferential head nod. "Director."

And then he was out the door, shutting it behind him with a soft click.

I was still staring at the stupid thing when Mariana started chuckling, her snide mirth practically begging me to launch her into outer space.

"And you're still here because?" I sniped.

"I'm still here because you have an assignment," she said matter-of-factly, like I was just supposed to hop-to and do her bidding.

"Assignment? Yeah, bitch, I don't work for you. I have a life I'd like to get back to. But you can take the runner-up prize of getting out of my house and never showing your face ever again. How about that?"

Mariana smiled so wide, I thought her face might crack. "And what's stopping me from putting your plea bargain in the shredder and terminating Killian's life? What's stopping me from tossing your boyfriend in jail? What, pray tell, is holding me back from wiping

Jeremiah's mind until he's a drooling mess on the floor? Or tossing that coven you care so much about into a hole just like I did your father?"

I opened my mouth to answer her, but she put up a hand. "No need for posturing, dear, it doesn't become you. I'll give you the answer. Nothing. Not one thing is stopping me. Except your compliance. Now, you might think that killing me will give you your desired outcome, but I assure you, it will not. I have plenty of people on my side who don't seem to like you very much. If anything were to happen to me, I guarantee they won't be as nice as I am. So..." She paused, letting me digest the grenade she just dropped on my life. "You have an assignment."

I was tempted to just see if she was telling the truth. I may not be an outright murderer—unless you counted Tabitha, and I didn't—but I was very interested in proving her theory.

Rather than setting her on fire, I did the super-adult thing and went to the kitchen. Crossing my fingers that Siobhan wasn't talking out of her ass about my fridge not being a rancid mess, I yanked open the freezer. Pleasantly surprised to find it fully stocked, I unearthed a bottle of vodka from under a bag of chicken nuggets and went about preparing a cocktail. I dumped a fair amount of the booze into a tall water glass along with some orange juice and a splash of cranberry. A quick stir later, and I was sipping my drink while I waited for Mariana to get the fucking lead out.

I should have known when I signed that agreement, she would figure out a way to fuck me over. After all she'd spilled about my real father, I should have figured she would try to keep me tethered. I mean... the man —*nope, not a man*—had murdered hundreds of people before they managed to put him down, imprisoning him under tons and tons of mountain.

And they'd only done that because they couldn't kill him. I suppose that was the fun fact about being the actual incarnate of death, dying wasn't on the menu for beings like that.

Yes, my father was the Angel of Death.

As if I didn't have enough problems.

Mariana rose from my chair and strode across the scant space, taking a seat at the bar. Like she'd done before, she waited in silence, trying to get me to fill the dead air. It hadn't worked before, and it wouldn't work now. I didn't want to talk to her. Hell, I didn't even want to look at her. She'd just threatened to imprison, maim, or murder literally everyone I cared about. What the fuck were we going to talk about? Smoothie recipes?

I continued to sip my vodka-laden juice, my patience wearing thin.

But not before hers.

She slapped a file onto the bar with a smack. Where she'd pulled it from was anyone's guess. She opened the folder and spun it for my inspection. I didn't bother looking at it.

"Your first assignment will be to solve these cold cases. There was a string of murders from 1995 through 2001 that have never been solved. Each victim was a fringe member of the arcane with little support. Since we didn't have a grave talker on staff at the time, nor did we have much to go on, the murders went cold. While it had been suggested that the cases were related, the evidence just isn't there."

I gave her my coldest glare. She wanted me to jump through fiery hoops with no more than a faint suggestion of a connection and exactly dick to go on? And I was, what, supposed to work on this in my spare time?

But Mariana wasn't done. Oh, no. She had more to say.

"I have already spoken to your captain. You are being lent to us for the time being. Though, he thinks we're the FBI and this is a fabulous opportunity for you."

I highly doubted that. Uncle Dave probably flipped off whomever he spoke to when they couldn't see. He hated the FBI almost as much as I hated the ABI, and he'd hate them too if he knew they existed.

"I will be keeping an eye on you while you complete this assignment. So, whatever you're planning in that little head of yours, stop it."

I actually hadn't been planning anything. I'd been practically tuning out her words while I studied her body language. People often lied with their lips, but their bodies didn't.

Everyone has a tell. Everyone.

Mariana's? She fought off a smile when she was exerting her power. She enjoyed being the big dog. Loved making sure people knew their place. She didn't need me to solve cases that were old enough to drink.

She wanted me under her thumb, spinning my wheels until I fell in line.

The fuck I would. I wouldn't be falling for that shit. Not ever.

My silence stretched longer and wider, my feigned indifference irking her more than if I'd spat in her face. Silence was my weapon of choice in several situations: it made criminals spill, it irked feds, it broke boyfriends. Now that I knew it pissed her off, it made my zipped lips that much sweeter.

Mariana let out a faint growl under her breath. "Contact Agent Kenzari about your access to our archives. You'll need them for these cases. I expect progress within twenty-four hours." Her smile grew wide. "Good luck."

With that, she stood and strode to the door. Before she crossed the threshold, she slipped a necklace over her head. With a wave of her fingers, the dark pendant glowed for a moment, and then Mariana's form melted away.

In her place was a short, mousey-looking woman with dishwater-blonde hair and horn-rimmed glasses. I'd scarcely wondered how she was going to "keep an eye on me." Especially in a town the size of Haunted Peak when she was supposed to be planted in the local cemetery. I now had my answer.

Fucking glamours.

"Oh, and Darby?" Mariana called like I wasn't staring right at her. "Stay away from Bishop La Roux. We wouldn't want anything bad to happen to him, now would we?"

With her parting shot, she strode right out my front door, slamming it behind her.

Mothers were the fucking worst.

4

I slammed back my cocktail in a single swallow. I hadn't been contemplating Mariana's demise, exactly. Maybe a punch to the face or perhaps an accidental immolation... But now? Oh, yeah, now I was out-and-out planning it. Not only did she need to go, but she needed to be launched into the surface of the sun at my earliest convenience.

I wondered if Shiloh St. James would help me with that. I was pretty sure if I told the Knoxville coven leader about what my mother had threatened, her whole coven would make sure Mariana had an "accident" and was never heard from again.

That gave me a small measure of happiness for about a solid minute before I started poking holes into the plan.

Who knew what Mariana had up her sleeve? This wasn't the woman from my childhood. This wasn't the sweet mom who bandaged my boo-boos and played hopscotch with me. She wasn't kind or soft. And I couldn't figure out if the woman from my past was real, or if I'd just made her up in the way kids did for an idolized parent.

I supposed I could ask my dad. If this was who my mother was now, I could see why he'd hidden her. Who wanted to crush their daughter's memories into dust? I knew I wouldn't have been able to do it if I had been in his shoes.

The sound of my back door opening had me reaching for a gun that most definitely was not on my hip. I was about to reach for a knife in the butcher block when J's voice hissed down the hall. "Is the coast clear?"

I let out a little bleat of laughter. "Yeah."

Frazzled-looking and more than a little pale, my partner, best friend, and closest confidant, Jeremiah Cooper raced into my kitchen. He didn't even say hi. Instead, he swiped the bottle of vodka and took a healthy swig.

J hadn't drunk vodka since the last bonfire party of our senior year of high school. That night he'd ended up fooling around with Greg Powell and lassoing himself a stage-five clinger who was so far in the closet, it might as well have been *Narnia*. J had sworn off all vodka drinks for the last decade because of that party. He was the sole reason I kept a bottle of gin right next to my vodka in the freezer.

"Well, hello to you, too," I muttered, my worry mounting after he took another pull of vodka. I snatched it away from him before he could drink any more, setting the bottle down on the counter and capping it.

J wiped his face before bracing himself against the counter like he might fall over. "I will happily get into the 'welcome backs' and all that shit in a minute, but only after you tell me why your grandfather is haunting my house. I about pissed myself this morning when he just popped up in my living room, and he hasn't made it easy to leave, either. What the fuck?"

Oh, shit. That totally explained why J looked like he was ready and willing to launch himself off a cliff.

"I may have told him he was no longer welcome in my house this morning," I mumbled with a wince.

"Say what now?" J's tone was way less frazzled as he moved for the vodka again.

I yanked it back out of his reach. "When I got out of ABI prison, he showed up acting like he wasn't the freaking reason I was there. So I socked him in the nose, and told him I didn't want to see him again."

J's face went from white to beet-red in an instant.

"*Prison?* That's where you've been this whole time. Fucking prison? Your mother put you in jail?"

I flicked off the cap of the vodka bottle and dumped some into my empty glass. "You've met my mother, J. The woman we grew up with is long gone. And it wasn't just prison. I also got poked and prodded and tested within an inch of my fucking life. Look," I muttered before taking a gulp of straight vodka. "You need to know that I have to work for her now. I don't know how long this is going to go on, but..."

J's pale-blue eyes went practically flinty. "She threatened us all, right? That's what Hildy said she'd do. He said a lot of shit, D. You really need to talk to him."

I caught myself mid-grumble. Just the thought of talking to Hildy made me want to rage. It was bad enough his daughter was the worst mother on the planet and deserved a painful death. But he was the one who was supposed to be on my side. He was the one who'd been with me day in and day out. He was the one who'd watched me wither away, drained to exhaustion.

He. Knew. And yet, he'd said nothing.

It was one thing to abandon me. It was quite another to pretend to be my friend and lie to my face.

"I don't want to talk to Hildy."

J turned his back to rummage in my freezer for his bottle of gin. At least one of us was thinking clearly. "I think he feels like shit for keeping his promise to her, and I have a feeling he'll be on our side. Plus, if you could get him out of my house, that would be awesome. I *seriously* about shit myself this morning, D. How in the high holy hell did you live with him for so long without losing your fucking mind?"

"Who says I haven't lost it? You're still my best friend, aren't you? I mean, if that doesn't make me *Looney Tunes*, I don't know what does."

J shot a withering glance over his shoulder before turning back to reach into my cupboard for a glass. "Get him out of my house, D. I'm not playing."

I stuck my tongue out at J behind his back. Childish, sure, but he couldn't see me.

"I saw that," he griped, his back still turned.

"You didn't see shit."

Groaning, I closed my eyes and called to Hildy in my mind. I imagined his pale hair and eyes, his paisley cravat and top hat, his skull cane and waistcoat. I pictured him sitting at my counter like he'd done nearly every day since I bought this house. I wondered how much power he'd used to show himself to J. It couldn't have been easy.

No, Darby. He lied to you. Don't go getting all soft now.

When I opened my eyes, Hildy was sitting exactly where I'd pictured him, a self-satisfied smile on his face.

"Don't make me hit you twice, Hildenbrand. Wipe that fucking smile off your face," I growled, my hands lighting up once again. They only seemed to do that in the presence of family. Go figure.

Given that my family was chock-full of assholes, it really made sense.

Hildy's face went serious. "I'm sorry, lass. It's just there has been very little joy since you left. I'm pleased to see you, that's all."

I scoffed and sipped my drink, doing my best not to smash it against the stone countertop when I was done. I was not falling for that guilt trip. Shuddering, I remembered the flash of a curved blade raking over my father's chest. That was pretty much all I'd dreamt about for the better part of a year. Well, that and Tabitha's malformed soul breaking free of her body.

Fighting off a full body freak-out, I settled on sarcasm. "What? Your other living family isn't a ball of sweetness and light? How weird."

"No, my sweet girl, they are not. Ya think I did ya a disservice by not telling ya about your powers, but... Ya got to grow up with a conscience and integrity. My children only grew up with the knowledge of power. Some of them died in their thirst for it. Others didn't. The ones who survived, aren't exactly the best of people. When ya came into your powers, I swore I would do it different. I'd show ya how to coexist with spirits, how to help them. Not use them for your own benefit."

My laugh was hysterical as I poured myself another glass of straight vodka. The room was a little spinny, but fuck it. I took another swig. "Absolute power corrupts absolutely. Lord Acton had it right."

"Mr. Cooper," Hildy called, and I looked up to see his form had mostly solidified on my barstool. "Please call for some take away. Darby needs sustenance if she's going to hear all I have to say."

J nearly choked on gin but gave my grandfather a nod. Hildy went see-through again, and it was then that I noticed the haggard quality to his face. He was using too much power.

"Where's your cane?" I asked, concern for the backstabber ingrained in my very DNA.

Hildy's lips stretched in a soft smile. "Stashed it so your mother couldn't find it. But that does leave me with not much power of my own."

"Then quit using so much, you idiot." I sighed and threw him a bone. "If you're going to stick around and help me send that bitch—no offense—packing, I need you to actually be useful."

Hildy perked up a bit. "You're going to let me stay?"

"Maybe. I'm still thinking about it. But no more secrets, Hildy. I'm serious. If I find out you're lying, I swear to everything holy, I won't just send you packing from my life."

Hildy's already-gray face went even paler. It wasn't an idle threat, and he knew it. Given who my father was, I could make sure Hildy never crossed into this plane again. Or... I was pretty sure I could.

"I'll do my best, lass. Living a life like mine, I've kept more secrets than I've told."

And that was as good as I was going to get, I supposed. Hildy had never been a fount of information—not about what I was, at least. Hell, he probably couldn't keep track of all the lies he'd told me over the years. What was there to do but accept this as my new reality?

I had a whole host of people in my life that I couldn't trust. My mother was a bitch in high heels, and my father had kept the fact that she was alive from me. Bishop was in the evil queen's back pocket, and I was stuck working for the hag.

My gaze fell on J. Well, I could trust at least one of them. Clearing my throat, I stuffed the ache down.

"Thai, Italian, or Indian?" I asked, reaching for the takeout menus.

J stared at the glasses full of booze, pursing his lips in concentration. "Italian. We need all the carbs we can get to soak this shit up." He raised a glass in the general direction where he'd last seen Hildy. "Okay, Gramps, time to spill it. What is Darby's ax-wound of a mother up to now?"

"My best guess? She's trying to find your siblings."

As drunk as I was, I was not, in fact, ready to have my world rocked to that degree. My mom had other kids? I had brothers or sisters? I was ill-prepared for the tears that gathered in my eyes and even less for the burn that smoldered in my chest.

I must have translated for Hildy because J piped up with a biting question.

"What? She lose track of all her children?" J asked sarcastically, probably not realizing that my mother was a few centuries old. She could have more kids. She could have fifty kids if she'd wanted to.

"Not hers," Hildy murmured, shaking his head. "His."

5

The Angel of Death had more than just one kid. Nope. My brain was not ready to wrap around that mess at all.

"Dude, you look like you're going to throw up," J said, replacing my glass of vodka with water. "Drink this and tell me what he said."

I gulped the ice-cold water down and prayed that my stomach decided not to eject what was in it. "She isn't looking for her own children," I croaked. "She's looking for *my father's* children."

Now it was time to come clean. I hadn't spoken to J since I'd been dumped in an ABI prison, so he didn't know what I did. He didn't know that I was ten times more of a freak than he'd originally signed on for when we were kids.

"You know what happened at the lake?" I hedged, trying to figure out just how to break the news to my best and only living friend in the world that I was... I was...

"Yeah." J's tone was wary. *Perfect.*

"You know the man Tabitha was trying to raise?" I asked, wincing.

"Are you sure you want to tell him, lass?" Hildy asked. "Knowing the truth isn't always the best thing for humans."

I shot Hildy a glare before J pulled on my shoulder, turning me to look at him.

"No way. That scary dude is your dad?"

I let out a hysterical little bleat of laughter. "Just wait. It gets better. This guy—who my mother liked enough to have a baby with—is the literal Angel of Death. So not only is my mother a grave talker and can talk to ghosts, but my father is the one who ferries them to their final resting place."

J's pale eyes popped wide as his jaw went slack.

Great. I'd broken him.

His head gave a sharp shake like he was trying to erase an Etch-A-Sketch. "If he's the one who takes everyone over to the other side, does that mean no one has made it over since he's been essentially buried under a fucking mountain for a couple of decades?"

Of course J would ask an intelligent question instead of freaking out. Since the day he'd decided to never let me go without backup, he'd been taking this arcane shit in stride.

"No. According to Mariana, he just has to be on Earth for people to make it over. I think that's why they didn't kill him for what he did. I can't imagine there being more ghosts cramming onto this tiny planet."

I shuddered at the thought. Ghosts who didn't move on in a timely manner turned bad fast. They lost themselves, got angry, and went from bland accountants and barbers to legit poltergeists. I couldn't imagine a whole world full of them. That sounded like a fucking nightmare.

J seemed confused. "What did he do? Why did they bury him?"

That wasn't a question I could answer exactly. I know what Mariana had told me he'd done, but the man I'd met didn't match up with the picture she painted. The man she described was a monster hell-bent on keeping his so-called throne. That didn't add up to the man who told me to put him back where he belonged. To the man who served Tabitha up to me on a silver platter. The man who had gone willingly back to his prison.

I'd met murderers and criminals. I saw them every day. I'd known men hardened by the sins on their soul, and no one learned their lesson that fast. Not after what she said he'd done.

"Mariana said he killed people. Hundreds of them. She said they were his children, and that he'd decided that he didn't want them anymore, that he regretted them all, and they... and he..." I broke off and took a gulp of water. "She said he killed his kids to keep his place. Not that I understand what that means."

"Jesus. You really got the short end of the stick in the parenting department," J mumbled.

I couldn't help but think he was absolutely right.

After consuming my weight in Spaghetti Carbonara and staying far, far away from the vodka, J and I dug into the case file Mariana had left for me. The information was thin, only the names, birth, and death dates, and the causes of death. No pictures, no leads, nothing else to give me even a measure of something to go on.

Fabulous.

"This isn't just thin evidence, this is practically anorexic. How in the blue fuck does she expect you to get anywhere with this?" J asked, exasperated at the sheer lack of investigative care anyone had taken on these cases.

"I'm supposed to contact Sarina to get into the

archives, but other than this flimsy shit, I have nothing." I looked to Hildy. "Do you think these people are still around? Like, could I call for them?"

Even as I asked the question, I knew it was a long shot. Ghosts without a purpose didn't tend to stick around. Hildy had family to haunt, others had unfinished business. Plus, I didn't even have a picture to go on to call them in my mind. I could search the DMV databases to see if anyone showed up, but some of these birthdates were several hundred years ago. It wasn't like I could just go look them up with that.

Hildy gave me a little hand waggle, meaning it would be a hard, if not impossible task. Ugh.

"Then that's what you have to do. She gave me her number if I needed anything. I have a feeling she really left it for you." J drew his phone from his back pocket and pulled up her contact, passing me the phone.

I hit the "Call" button and waited about half a ring before she answered. "Well, if it isn't my favorite grave talker. How are ya, Darby?"

Sarina Kenzari was one of my favorite people to come out of the ABI. Tiny, straightforward, and a little bit of a nut, Sarina didn't fit into the mold I'd conjured in my head about what an ABI agent should be.

"Trust an oracle to know who is on the other end of the phone, right? You know why I'm calling, too?"

Sarina snorted. "Of course. I've already made you an access badge and everything. I suggest you get here as soon as you can. You don't have much time."

"Why does she need movement on these cases? Some of them are over twenty years old." It was a question that had been bugging me since Mariana handed me the file. Something had put this bee in her bonnet, and I wanted to know what it was.

Sarina sighed, and I could practically feel the exasperation in the gust from here. "I can't say. But you should get Killian to drive you. You've had way too much vodka to get behind the wheel."

Groaning, I stomped my foot like a child. "But I'm not ready to talk to him yet. Don't you want to come get me? We could gab about what you've been up to for the last nine months while I was rotting away in Hotel Hell."

She chuckled, but I could feel her answer before she gave it. "Can't, babe. I have to babysit a pissed-off death mage, and pray he doesn't do some dumb shit on my watch. Trust me, I'd much rather be dealing with you than him. But we do need to have a conversation—and soon. Just get here."

I had to wonder what had Bishop all riled up—other than my mother, that was.

"Fine," I grumbled petulantly. "See you soon."

I ended the call and slapped J's phone in his hand before crawling to the island. Pulling myself up, I groaned again. "I left my personal effects in Bishop's car."

Perfect. Just perfect. I'd have to buy a new phone and pray I'd remembered to back up the old one sometime before I'd been sent off to become an ABI lab rat.

"Personal effects?" J asked. "They wouldn't happen to be in a giant Zip-Lock with clothes in it, would they? Because I saw something like that on your back porch."

Frowning, I went to inspect the mystery bag, and it indeed was the plastic bag I'd left in Bishop's truck. He'd remembered and circled back. I tried not to put so much stock in a simple kind gesture, but it was difficult. Everything about Bishop screamed "stay away," while also daring someone as inquisitive as I was to come closer.

It wasn't that he was shifty because he wasn't. It was that he was a mystery to be solved, and secret to uncover, an entire ball of yarn to untangle, and I wanted that so bad I could taste it. But I didn't know if I could trust Bishop's allegiances, and moreover? I didn't know who he'd choose if it came down to it.

I opened the bag on the way back to my kitchen and fished out my phone. Naturally, it was off, but I managed to turn it on. Plugging it in for good measure, I debated on whether or not I wanted to call my father. A part of me practically died wanting to talk to him, and the other wanted to sock him in the face. And then there was this whole other part that wanted to know why.

Why had he kept her lie a secret? Why had he pretended like I was a normal girl? Why hadn't he told me that he knew what I was?

I wasn't going to get my answers by just staring at my phone, that was for damn sure. Reluctantly, I picked the phone up off the counter and went to my "Last Dialed," ignoring the literal thousands of email notifications and incoming missed texts.

When I hit the "Call" button, I nearly hung the phone right back up. What the hell was I going to say?

"Darby?" my father answered on the first ring, like he'd been waiting for me to call.

"Yeah, Dad." My voice was little more than a croak. The last time I'd seen him, he'd just taken his first breath since… I couldn't even think about it.

"Oh, my sweet baby girl. Can I come over? Can I… My god, Darby, I missed you so much."

And then I was crying on the phone, blubbering to my daddy like a five-year-old with a boo-boo. "I missed you, too."

"I'm coming over, okay. Is that okay?"

"Yeah," I squeaked, unable to say anything else. I'd

dreamt about Tabitha murdering him every night. About the flash of her knife.

In my nightmares, he never came back. Bishop and I had been too late, or Tabitha couldn't be killed, or the monster hiding under her flesh had ripped me to shreds. The endings were always different, but the outcome was the same. I'd failed my dad. I'd failed everyone.

"I love you, Darby. I'll see you in a minute."

"Love you, too," I croaked, my voice like broken glass. It was hard not to feel the relief of him being whole again, but I knew I wouldn't believe it was real until I saw him with my own two eyes.

Why hadn't I stopped at my dad's house first? Why did I wait? I was so stupid, letting my anger keep me away when his life was so short. Compared to the life I was estimated to have, his time on this earth was a mere blink. I could lose him at any second, really. He could trip *Final Destination* style and fall down the stairs or get in an accident.

Or my life, my being just in his general vicinity, could bring death to his doorstep.

Again.

The loss that I'd so narrowly avoided hit me like a brick. I could work cases because I was removed from death in a way no one else was. I saw it all the time; I heard it every day. I was in it up to my neck, and when you were in it, you didn't see it anymore. Death hung around me like a cloud. I ate, slept, and breathed it.

But I'd never lost anyone I really cared about except for my mother.

She couldn't take his life away. She couldn't rip him from me like Tabitha had.

Gulping down my tears, I made my way to the bathroom. I knew J and Hildy probably didn't understand, but that didn't really matter right now.

Well, maybe Hildy would, but I doubted it.

I needed to get my shit together, hug my dad, and get this investigation under my belt.

Then, I was going to bury Mariana Adler if it was the last thing I did.

6

It took far too long for me to get my shit tight enough to come out of the bathroom. I was not a pretty crier, and the evidence of my mini mental breakdown was stamped on my face for the world to see.

Puffy eyes? Check.

Blotchy skin? Check.

Nose red enough to give Rudolph a run for his money? Check.

I was gorgeous, I tell you. Gorgeous!

But me in all my puffy, red glory did not matter one little bit to my dad. As soon as I extricated myself from the safety of my bathroom, Dad left J at the door and wrapped me up in a bear hug so tight I could barely breathe.

I didn't give that first shit.

He smelled like he always had: aftershave, leather, and a faint hint of pipe tobacco. It was all I could do not to dissolve into a mess of tears as I hugged him back as tight as I could.

"I missed you, kid. I missed you a whole bunch," he murmured into my hair before setting me back on my feet.

I brushed wayward tears off my face. "Jesus, who the fuck is cutting onions in here?"

My father let out a bark of laughter as he threw an arm around my shoulders. "I'm glad to see you here safe, Darby."

"Ditto, you big dope. Have you been doing okay?"

I didn't know the side effects of being brought back from the dead, but I had to assume they weren't a picnic. I worried about him every single day while I was gone. And yes, I simultaneously wanted to punch him in the face, but that was neither here nor there.

"As well as could be expected. Your mother told me where you were, and I worried about you every day, sweetheart. I never wanted this life for you, never wanted you in danger like this. I hope you understand that was the only reason I kept everything a secret."

I tried not to rage at the simplicity of that statement. He hadn't wanted me to be in danger, but hadn't said that first word when I'd applied for the police academy after college. When I'd broken up bar fights and frat parties and domestic violence cases. All the while trying to deny an intrinsic part of myself so hard, I'd almost gone insane.

I stepped out from under his arm and backed up a few paces. I couldn't be hugged while I dropped this truth bomb. "I know you'd like to think you were doing the right thing, Dad. But you had to have seen me floundering. You had to have known what was happening. If you knew about my mother, you had to have realized I was like her. You knew what she was, knew she wasn't dead, and I was hurting. You left me adrift to figure out my life and my abilities all on my own. You let me believe she was dead."

My father opened his mouth, but I held up a hand to stop him. "I know she's a bitch on wheels with spinning fucking rims. I get it. But I thought I was going crazy. And you left me to that. We are not square, Dad. I'm mad as hell at you for knowing and not saying anything. But I love you, and I'm glad you're alive, and I'm glad you raised me and not her."

My father looked like I'd punched him in the gut, but I refused to feel bad about what I'd just said.

I would throw him a bone, though. "I don't have many people in my life that I can just be me around. If you don't mind me occasionally looking like I'm talking to people who don't seem to be there, that would go a long way."

Dad blinked at me hard for a moment as his face went white. A realization seemed to cross his face, with shame following swiftly after. Tears swam in his eyes for a moment before he closed them and took a deep breath.

"What you ask of me is the bare minimum of what I should be doing. I'm so sorry I failed you, kid."

It was a struggle not to tell him it was okay. That he was a good dad. He was—especially compared to Mariana. Hell, compared to my mother, he would win father of the universe. But this was a lesson that needed to be learned.

"I accept your apology."

He'd been the one to teach me that. That when someone hurt you, you couldn't just say "it's okay" because it wasn't. "It's okay" told people that they could do it again. That you weren't mad. That there was no real consequence for hurting you.

At my response, Dad smiled, his memory of the lesson just as fresh as mine.

"So, J says you need a ride?"

The drive to the Knoxville ABI office wasn't as long as I would have liked. Being in my father's presence was a balm to my soul, even if J and Hildy were riding in the back seat.

"So where does everyone else think I've been for the last nine months?" I asked. Mariana hadn't been clear, and I didn't expect her to cover for me while I was in arcane prison. Although J had told me about the bullshit "FBI gig," I wondered if there was another story floating around.

Dad shot me a sidelong glance before turning his eyes back to the road. "Working for the FBI on a big case. Apparently, your expertise has been invaluable to them, and you've been requested to extend your tenure indefinitely. Your mother smoothed it over for you. Uncle Dave has no idea where you really were."

I snorted. Extend my tenure indefinitely. *Yeah, right.* Not if I could help it.

"And the mayor? What does everyone think happened there? Tabitha? Suzette? What's the scoop?" J and I hadn't gone too in depth in our booze-fueled dive into the ABI files.

"Murder-suicide. As far as anyone knows, Suzette and Duncan were having undisclosed marital problems, and they had it out. It was splashed all over everywhere for weeks. Tabitha went on 'sabbatical,' and Blair Simpkins murder is still unsolved. Funnily enough, the homicide rate in Haunted Peak has gone down considerably since Tabitha went on her little walkabout."

It hurt how close to the truth some of that was. Suzette Duvall had killed her husband, and in a way, trying to raise the Angel of Death was a great way to kill yourself. If not clean, it sure was unique. It was Tabitha's sabbatical that irked me. No one would know what she had done, because the lone murder I could likely prove was my father's. Him not being dead anymore kind of put a kink in my case.

I still didn't feel sorry for killing Tabitha, but my lack of remorse didn't really sit well with me. I was a bona fide murderer, even if the woman I'd killed hadn't been human. Could I be a good cop when I didn't care that I'd taken her life?

A flash of her knife streaked across my brain. Nope. Still not sorry.

"What do you expect to find in the archives?" J asked, breaking me out of my Tabitha-fueled mini-shame spiral.

I thought about it for a moment. "Real names and birthdates. Pictures. If I'm going to summon them, I need something to go on. From there, I hope to get at least one of them to talk to me."

Even if it was a total long shot. Specters deteriorated quite quickly when they didn't have something or someone to stick around for. If they did have that tie that would keep them on this plane, they might not come when I summoned them.

Or they might not even be lucid.

Honestly, this whole thing was a crapshoot, and I was probably going to fail.

Great attitude, Darby. Way to rise to the occasion.

I mentally gave my bitchy self the finger.

"Do you think that'll work? Don't you usually work with fresher spirits?" J asked, echoing my doom and gloom.

I sighed, rubbing my temple. Exhaustion was creeping in, and I knew what it was. I hadn't been around ghosts in almost a year. Even as juiced up as I still was, Hildy's proximity was getting to me. Well, that and the glass of straight vodka probably hadn't helped, either.

"Fresher spirits?" Dad echoed, and my brain worked overtime to try and figure out how to explain just how I had the highest close rate in the county.

"I see and talk to ghosts, Dad. And I'm very good at questioning witnesses."

Dad let out a bark of laughter. "No wonder. I thought that might be it, but you hide it so well, I didn't know if you blocked them out or what. What better witness than the person who was killed. Jesus Christ on a saltine cracker."

I shrugged in my seat, my cheeks going hot. "One would think the victim would be a solid witness, right? Not so much. But they do give me good intel, and I have a pretty great partner."

Dad chuckled, J laughed, and I rubbed my temple again.

It was going to be a long day.

Arriving at the address Sarina supplied via text, I realized a few things. One, my outfit of jeans and a Green Day T-shirt were going to go over like a lead balloon. A few agents came in and out of the front doors like they owned the place. Their suits and shiny shoes and crisp demeanor surrounding them like a cloud of indifference. Two, J wouldn't be able to go with me. That text came not a second before Dad pulled up to the front of the building. Sarina's "sorry" was not the balm she likely had meant it to be. And three? I was not at all happy about being here. There was something foreboding about this building, and it had nothing to do with ghosts.

First of all, there weren't any. Not a single spirit, specter, or apparition clung to the place. It was as if the wardings also had a "Stay Back Fifty Feet" sign on them. So not only was J not going to come, Hildy likely wouldn't make it through the front door, either.

That meant that in the event they didn't let me out, I didn't have an extra power source to change their minds.

Fuck.

I swallowed hard and shot Hildy a knowing glance. His face was grayer than usual, the haggard lines of strain etched into his nearly see-through skin.

"Go get your cane, Hildenbrand. You can't help me if you drain yourself dry."

Hildy's smile was grateful. "All right, lass. All right."

He winked out of sight, and I was left staring at the other two men in the car who didn't seem to realize they'd been traveling with a ghost this entire time.

"What? Hildy follows me damn near everywhere."

Dad's face slowly but surely regained color, and J kept staring at the seat next to him as if it might rise up to bite him on the nose. I had to wonder what Hildy had done to him during his stay at J's house.

"I have to go in alone, guys. I'll call you when I can come home."

It was an empty promise. I had no idea if I was ever making it out again.

7

By the time I had peeled myself from my father's car, Sarina was on the front steps of the giant gray building. Agent Sarina Kenzari was a tiny ball of energy, her short black bob swaying as she bounded down the steps to collect me.

"I'm so glad to see you," she squealed, and without warning, she threw her arms around me, wrapping me up in a hug so tight, I feared for the state of my lungs. I was not a hugger. I appreciated them, but my awkwardness was on a level heretofore measured by modern science.

"Good to see you, too," I muttered warily, wondering if I would make it out of the hug intact.

"Okay, fine, spoilsport. No hugs. I wouldn't want to offend your delicate sensibilities."

I'd forgotten how odd it was to have Sarina in my space. The oracle had solid telepathic abilities which made it easier to ghost translate, but super weird when it came to keeping my mind private.

"I'm not going to get stuck in there, am I?" I asked before she could read the worries stamped all over my thoughts. "You don't have shackles on standby, right?"

Sarina shot me an odd expression. On anyone else, it would read as confusion, but I doubted Sarina had been confused a day in her life.

"You honestly believe that with all the power you have underneath your skin that anyone at any time could trap you?" she asked, her voice barely a whisper as if she were worried she'd be overheard.

"That's not an answer, and you know it. And you and I both know that I can be trapped in other ways."

Mariana threatening my family and friends being the primary incentive to stay put.

Sarina's confusion morphed to understanding. "Ah. That makes more sense."

Again, not an answer, but I doubted Sarina could give me one.

"Come on, D," she instructed, using J's abbreviation of my name. "You've got an archive room to scour."

The ABI office appeared like any other federal building: gray cinderblock walls, bad fluorescent lighting, and the stale scent of burnt coffee wafting through the hallways. I didn't know if this building was the same one I'd been interrogated in before my joyous stay in Hotel Hell or not, but mostly, it felt the same. This entrance being topside didn't mean anything. It could be the public front while the real work and offices were held elsewhere.

I saw very few people in the halls, but I felt more behind closed doors, milling about out of sight. Weirdly, that ability hadn't faded much since the last time I'd been in a building like this one. It seemed that sense had only been muted by the wards in the prison, and time had no hold on it.

After the events up at Whisper Lake, the normal buzzing I felt every day was dialed up to eleven. I knew where souls were up to a few miles away, and I knew how they were dying if they were close to that. I could feel them like ants on my skin, and that odd sensation hadn't dimmed too much.

Funny, I hadn't realized it earlier. Was that ability going on the fritz? Or was I ignoring it?

I followed Sarina to a green-gray elevator, and she pressed a floor labeled "B2."

Sub-basements. Joy.

My anxiety of being trapped in this building for the rest of my days ramped up with each floor—all three of them—

that we passed, burying me deeper and deeper underground. All the while, Sarina kept chattering on about ID badges and access and where we were going next. I vaguely recalled how to walk as she led me to a caged file room and unearthed a large golden key from her pocket.

I must have made a noise because Sarina was right in front of me, her small hands digging into the tops of my shoulders.

"Darby? It's okay. You don't have to go in. There is an attendant here who will pull what you need. You aren't going to be locked in, babe. I swear."

I hadn't thought being in the ABI facility for nine months had changed me at all. Hadn't contemplated what—if anything—was different about being in prison for such a short time. But now I knew why so many former prisoners vowed to never go back. Because just the thought of being locked up again made me want to run screaming from this building.

Somehow, I managed to get a lock on my fear. Maybe it was the feeling of Sarina's soul—which had been a muted buzz before but was now a singing beacon in my brain. Maybe it was the promise in her words, and the knowledge she'd given me on the steps.

With as much power as you have under your skin, do you really think anyone at any time could trap you?

No one was going to keep me if I didn't want to be kept. No one was going to cage me. Not ever again. I wasn't going to be here forever, just as long as I remembered that I was going to be okay.

I was.

Right?

"I'm okay," I croaked, swallowing hard as I got my heartrate somewhere in the normal range. "I can go in." With a few cleansing breaths and a mantra of vile deaths for anyone who would cage me, I managed to peel myself from the cinderblock wall and follow Sarina into the archives cage.

Farther in the room was a sad gray desk and a man slumped in his chair with his head resting on his fist, sleeping. Complete with a stained button-up shirt, loose tie, and a bad combover, the pitiful-looking records keeper was snoring away at his desk, oblivious in his sleep at our arrival.

"Kevin," Sarina called, but he snored on. "Kevin," she hissed, clunking the desk with her black combat boot.

Kevin sputtered awake, his mousey-brown combover sliding comically off his forehead to expose the bald patch underneath. His watery blue eyes were bloodshot as he blearily stared up at Sarina. I figured he would be a cranky sort, but he seemed to have a soft spot for my tiny friend.

"A-Agent Kenzari," Kevin said, reverence in his every word. He sat up straighter and fiddled with his tie. "How can I help you today?"

Sarina gave him a practically beatific smile and gestured to me. "Kevin, I want you to meet Darby Adler. She's working on a mountain of cold cases, and I want you to help her in every way you can."

I gave Kevin a truncated wave, but he didn't even spare me a glance.

"Absolutely." Kevin sighed dreamily and propped his head on his hand. "Anything for you."

Oh, dear. Poor Kevin was positively smitten and had less than no shot.

"You're a doll, Kevin," Sarina cooed, hamming it up. "Do me an extra favor?"

"Anything," he breathed, and it was all I could do not to giggle. Honestly, Kevin was freaking adorable.

"Keep the cage open? Darby has a thing about small spaces."

Kevin gave me an appraising onceover at Sarina's statement, an expression of kindness sweeping his features before he wiped it away. "No problem."

With that, Sarina bid the both of us a quick goodbye, leaving me with the love-struck Kevin who was staring after her like she'd reappear at any moment.

"It's nice to meet you," I said, doing my best not to make any new enemies while I was here.

Kevin startled and shot his gaze back to me. "Good to meet you, too. So, they got you on cold case duty. That must suck."

I shrugged. "It's in my skill set, I guess."

I mean, who else is going to be able to solve old cases except for someone who can talk to ghosts?

Kevin's eyes popped wide, and I guessed that little bit came out of my mouth. Whoops.

"You're a grave talker? You're not that woman who..." Kevin trailed off, his face going positively white.

Greeeeaaaaat. I had a reputation.

I fought off the urge to bow. "I'm not sure what you've heard, but I'm nice, I swear. I just want to do this job and not be stuck down here for the rest of forever." I paused, hearing the words and how they must have sounded to him. "Not that there is anything wrong with being down here, it's just—"

Kevin waved away my fumbling explanation. "Don't worry about it. I get it. A lot of people don't like being underground. I know you didn't mean anything by it. It's good to meet you, Darby. Let's get you what you need."

A few dozen files later, I was elbow-deep in names, birthdates, and gruesome crime scene photos. The photos weren't the best quality, and it made me miss Jimmy something fierce.

I had known Jimmy, the best crime scene photographer in the world, since we were kids. Granted, I hadn't known he was part elf at the time, but it totally explained the long hair he used to get shit over in school. I missed my desk and my office supplies. Missed my process.

Now I had a rickety chair and plain yellow post-its and a mountain of unruly data.

The first file was a woman by the name of Donna Sherwood. She'd died in 1995 at the ripe old age of three hundred and seven. Donna could have passed for a soccer mom, her pin-straight blonde bob a thing of beauty. But her identification photo was nothing compared to the gruesome death scene. According to the photos—and the scarcely filled-out reports—Donna had been torn apart by a shifter of some kind. So had her children and husband and family fucking dog. The records vaguely pointed to her being a witch of some kind, but she hadn't had a coven to speak of.

The detective work was shit, absolute shit. Time of death hadn't been established until a week later, and the medical examiner's paperwork was sloppy and incomplete.

The next file was for Ferris Laramie, a blood mage that had been found at the bottom of a ravine in 1997. His death had been ruled accidental, but it didn't add up. He'd had peri-mortem bruising that had been identified but dismissed, and a boatload of cries from his husband about foul play. He, too, wasn't a member of a coven and didn't have many friends. Born in the 1550s, Ferris' records of his life prior to the century he'd died were scant. Just like the one I held in my hands.

On and on it went. Each person died of unusual or outright violent circumstances, with little evidence, little investigation, and shoddy policework.

I tried to see if the same investigator had been on all the cases but hit a dead end. I knew it would be too easy to pin it on one lone ABI agent and call it a day.

I was engrossed in my work when a man's voice damn near startled me out of my seat.

"I didn't realize the fresh meat would be so pretty."

Whipping my head up, I spied a frat boy ABI agent, attempting the nonchalant pose of resting his shoulder on the wall. Sandy-blond hair, green eyes, chiseled jaw, the suited man seemed false in almost every way. His face was a mask of feigned innocence, like he hadn't just been a whole-ass sleaze, while his posture spoke of a fake sort of calm.

He'd called me fresh meat. Like I was chum in the water and he was the shark.

"I didn't realize ABI shitbags would be so sleazy," I shot back. "Gotta love quippy sexual harassment on my first day. How ever will I survive without it?"

I rolled my eyes and turned back to my work, fighting off the urge to let him know how many ways I could murder him in this tiny tucked-away corner.

Stupidly, the douche approached, piercing my bubble like the creepy creep he was. "Oh, don't be like that. I was just joking."

My mouth popped off without consulting my brain, but the bitch did have some really good things to say. "I wasn't, and I didn't take it that way. And just so we're clear, I'll slit your stupid throat and leave you to bleed out in a dark corner somewhere with exactly zero remorse. Mm-kay, Pumpkin?"

I probably wouldn't, but this idiot didn't know that.

"They said you were a feisty one, but they have no idea, do they?"

Did this fucker miss the imminent threat to his life, or was he just stupid? Without much prompting on my part, my hands began to glow, the heat of them a comforting balm to my nerves. I stood slowly from my evil chair, realizing very quickly that he was my height.

"Quick question there, hoss. Do you think I give two shits what you think about me?"

His eyes widened as he stared at my glowing hands. I wasn't a hundred percent on what I could do to a living soul, but he was making me ache to find out.

"Um, Darby?" Kevin called from the door the agent just vacated. "Agent Kenzari requested that you not kill Agent Easton. She said it was too much paperwork and she was busy."

I snorted out an indelicate laugh while both Kevin and Easton stared at me with wide, frightened eyes.

My glow ramped down, and I met Easton's gaze. "Lucky you," I said, my smile positively gleeful as his face went from shocked to ashen. Did I show him all my teeth as I smiled? Maybe. I turned to Kevin, but he cut me off.

"She said to take your files to the fourth floor, and she'd collect you at the elevator."

I nodded, glad for Sarina in all her oracle glory.

I stacked the files in my arms, leaving both Kevin and Easton in my dust.

8

Finding the elevator wasn't easy. I wasn't thinking very clearly when Sarina and I had descended to the second basement level, and I couldn't remember which turn I was supposed to take. It took a few wrong turns and retracing my steps, but finally, I was on my way to the fourth floor.

With a giant stack of files in my arms, I pressed the appropriate floor button and tried not to drop my quarry. I needed this information—as scant and full of holes as it was—to get anywhere on this case. But as soon as the elevator dinged its arrival at the appropriate floor and the door slowly slid open, all hell broke loose.

I was barely out of the elevator car before red lights flashed in the hallway. An alarm sounded, and I could have sworn the thing was a World War II movie air-raid siren. And it wasn't Sarina waiting for me.

It was Bishop.

Well, he wasn't waiting exactly. He was running at me full tilt. Before I could back up, he was grabbing me and yanking me by the arm to a stairwell. I barely held onto the files as I followed him down the concrete steps.

"What's going on?" I screamed to be heard over the alarm. But Bishop didn't deign to answer me. Instead, he jerked the files out of my arms, shoving them into a bag he'd conjured from thin fucking air and shouldering it before snagging my hand. I suppose it wouldn't have mattered. I could barely hear myself. There was no way I'd have been able to hear him.

On the second floor, Bishop muscled a door open—a door that didn't look like it should be there at all. Hidden in the lines of the cinderblock, the secret door seemed to go to nowhere, a blackness so dark it looked like the mouth to Hell. I tried to pull back, but Bishop just yanked me harder after him. When it closed behind us, the alarm went silent. Or maybe since we just went through a door to fucking who knew where, we weren't in the building anymore.

Panic threatened to swallow me up, and it was all I could do to keep my feet moving as Bishop pulled me to a place I couldn't see.

"Darby?" Bishop called, and it was a struggle to calm my breathing enough to answer him.

"What?" I hissed, going for bravado rather than blind panic.

"We were breached—the building. And not just breached. The ABI is under attack."

Under attack?

"What about Sarina? What about the other agents? Did they make it out?" I asked, the hysteria not entirely out of my voice. Okay, I was one high squeak away from a padded cell, but whatever.

Bishop tightened his grip on my hand and pulled me faster. "She sent me to get you. She's fine."

Even in my fractured state, I still totally caught that he in no way answered my question. "That's not an answer, La Roux, and you damn well know it."

"Yeah, I know," he muttered under his breath before pulling me to a stop. "Don't move. Don't even breathe. Understand?"

I squeezed his hand in answer, and he let me go. A faint trace of purple magic lit what I hoped were his hands, swirling around and around before flying off his fingers in an arc. The magic exploded against a barrier— a wall, maybe—flowing outward until it found what it was looking for. The magic flowed like water into a crevasse, forming a line that quickly morphed into a rectangle.

The rectangle began to glow, and with its light, I could make Bishop out in the dim. He lurched forward and grabbed a metal doorknob, cracking the door just enough that he could inspect what was on the other side. When he was satisfied, he reached for me, hauling us both through the door before slamming it shut behind us.

Springtime heat hit me square in the face as we emerged into a quirky-looking alley. The brick façade was painted with cheerful colors. Murals of children playing and families embracing reminded me of a particular part of Knoxville that I'd visited more than a few times. Peals of giggles echoed off the brick, the sound sending a shockwave of relief through my system. We were safe. I knew this place.

This was close to the coffee shop where I'd met Shiloh last year.

There were a few places in Knoxville that were reserved for the arcane world. Areas where the humans didn't venture on their own without a damn good reason. This was one of those places.

"We need to move," Bishop hissed, the giggles not as comforting to him as they were to me. "If we're caught here, we're fucked."

I couldn't understand why he, of all people, would be afraid of this neighborhood. Sure, it was full of arcaners, but so were a lot of places. Unless...

"Please tell me you aren't on the outs with—"

"Well, well, well," a childlike voice called from the mouth of the alley. "What do we have here?"

Bishop cursed long and low under his breath. His shoulders seemed to crawl up to his ears as he braced himself, tugging me behind him.

I stared around Bishop's shoulder and down the mouth of the alley where what seemed like a little girl was barring our way. She appeared no older than eight, with plaited blonde hair and a schoolgirl's uniform on her tiny frame. But I knew the crest on her jacket didn't belong to any school.

Oh, no.

No, the little girl at the end of the alley was in no way human, and that crest on her jacket was for her nest, not for a hoity-toity school. She might be hiding her red eyes and needlelike fangs, but that didn't make her any less dangerous.

"Darby Adler, what are you doing slumming it with the ABI shitbag? I thought I taught you better than that," she said, her smile showing a peek of fang.

At her words, Bishop froze, his head turning slowly to appraise me. I simply shrugged. He knew I'd had an in with nearly every arcane group in the city. Hell, I'd saved their asses more times than I could count.

And this not-so-little girl? Yeah, she owed me big.

Ingrid Dubois was the Dubois nest enforcer. To hear her tell it, she'd been a vampire since before the fall of Rome. Personally, it creeped me the fuck out to know that someone had turned a child. Especially since I knew what the spell for turning entailed. But Ingrid didn't seem to mind her small stature or unassuming appearance.

She reveled in it.

Skirting around Bishop, I approached the tiny-yet-deadly vamp, opening an arm for a hug. I usually wasn't a hugger, but I did so love to freak Bishop out, and me hugging an ancient vampire was sure to send him into a fit.

"You know how it is, Ing. One day you're stuck in prison, the next, you're on the run from an attack. It's the life, right?"

Ingrid gave me a little squeeze, careful not to hurt me, and pulled back. "Yeah, that's half the reason I'm out on patrol."

The other half—she didn't need to tell me—was that she loved making sure her queen was protected, and a general's place was on the ground.

"What do you mean?" Bishop broke in, not realizing

that Ingrid's hospitality did not extend to him. Or maybe he did. Bishop knew just from Ingrid's giggle that he was in deep shit. To me, her laugh was a sign I was in the right place.

To him, it was clearly a signal he was fucked. What had he done to get on Ingrid's bad side?

She shot him a withering glare before turning back to me. "We heard about the attack. Word is, it was a bunch of un-nested vamps who did it. I swear, the last thing we need is the ABI up our asses, and this is a sure-fire way to bring that heat. I swear to fucking Christ himself that if this hurts my queen, things are gonna get dicey."

It still cracked me up that Ingrid looked about eight years old but had the mouth of a well-seasoned trucker with a solid sailor dialect to boot.

"I didn't know there were un-nested vamps in the city," I admitted, wondering how much had changed since I'd been locked up. "I thought that was, you know, frowned upon?"

I knew it was more than frowned upon. The ABI was strict as hell about ghouls and vampires being un-nested. There was an approval process, and most just got locked up on general principle. If a vampire or a ghoul was too feral to be in a nest, they had some serious issues and shouldn't mix with the mundane public.

"Yeah. Well, things have changed since you've been gone. Stuff's getting weird. A few months ago, there was an attack just up the road in Ascension. Nested ghouls attacking other arcaners with no real reason why. It didn't make any sense then, and it sure as shit doesn't make any now."

I shot a look at Bishop. Why hadn't he told me about this?

"Don't look at me like that. I was just excited to have you free. I didn't think I wouldn't have the time to say anything. A lot has happened, Darby. A lot."

Ingrid huffed. "I thought you just loved to spill, La Roux. Isn't that what you're known for?"

Bishop rolled his eyes. "Oh, come on. You can't still be blaming me for Thomas leaving. I saved his stupid life. You *should* be thanking me."

I'd heard Ingrid wax poetic about her favorite nestmate Thomas. He'd left the Dubois nest a century before I was even a twinkle in my dad's eye.

Holy shit. I shot an appraising glance to Bishop. "You're the reason Ingrid hates the ABI? Sweet lord, man. And she let you live? To hear Ingrid tell it, you broke into their coven and hauled Thomas off, ne'er to be heard from again."

Bishop growled. "I didn't break in, for fuck's sake. I knocked on the damn door. I'd heard word that his birth nest had an assassin in town and might have infiltrated his home. I was doing him a favor. Unless you forgot, I saved his life. It's not my fault your screening process was shit. Probably still is." He said that last bit under his breath, but being what she was, Ingrid still heard him.

Her pale-gold eyes went scarlet in an instant.

"Oh, wait," Bishop said sarcastically, "aren't *you* in charge of that?"

Ingrid practically vibrated with rage, and it was all I could do to step between them before she snapped him like a twig. I was half-tempted to yank Bishop by the ear and make him sit in the corner.

"Whoa, whoa, whoa, guys. No need for name-calling. Past beefs can be tabled for the foreseeable future until we figure out why the ABI building got attacked. No one wants the ABI in the middle of day-to-day affairs less than me, so why don't we try to figure this out?"

Ingrid glared around me at the likely equally pissed-off death mage. I could practically feel the rage wafting off of both of them.

"Fine, but not here," Ingrid growled, her elfin face slowly dialing back from blind fury. "Buckle up, Death Boy. We're going to the nest."

9

The Dubois nest was like something out of a '90s goth movie. If "vampire" had an aesthetic, it was this place. Housed in one of the few gothic-style churches in Knoxville, the nest was filled with black-wearing, pale-faced people scurrying around like the light actually hurt them.

It didn't.

It was a myth that sunlight burned vampires to a crisp. A tale that had been perpetuated by the vamps themselves because it kept their secret. Not that in this day and age keeping the secret was really the top priority. With as many movies and TV shows that featured vamps, they could pretty much walk among the masses undetected. According to a few of my sources, the Spanish Inquisition had been a rough time, but nowadays?

It was freaking paradise.

The same went for crosses, holy water, and all forms of religious paraphernalia. The only real thing that hurt a vamp was a beheading or a stake to the heart. But truth be told? Nearly everything died if you made their heart stop beating.

Well, except for ghouls, but that was another story altogether.

The Dubois nest home was small compared to others in the States, but it was one of the few that didn't require all members to live in-house. The New England and Pacific Northwest nests were run by less-than-innovative monarchs with little to no interest in progressing with the times. The old ways required everyone to live together, and the drama that entailed was exhausting—or so I'd heard.

The Knoxville vampire queen was not a fan of drama, bullshit, or games. Not even a little.

Ingrid led Bishop and I through the giant cathedral, the lectern set up like the throne it most definitely was. Sitting at the top was a dark-haired woman that could pass for twenty if she was a day. Icy-pale skin contrasted beautifully with her carefully coiffed hair and deep-red lipstick.

She wore a jeweled crown on her head and a dress that probably cost more than I made in ten years. There were tiny rubies sewn into the fabric of her coal-black dress, making it shimmer like fresh blood, which was the probable intent. But it was her eyes that told of her real age. Typically, vampires had what I called a "human" look and a "phased" look. If they weren't feeding, pissed off, or in the middle of "happy time," most vampires could pass for human if you didn't know what to look for. But phased vampires were a whole other animal. Phased, they had a secondary set of needles for fangs and solid red eyes that told of blood and death and a whole host of not good things.

If Ingrid was old, Magdalena Dubois was ancient.

"Detective Darby Adler and an ABI fuck-stick, my queen," Ingrid announced while bowing slightly once we'd reached the end of the aisle.

I gave the queen a short head bow, but Bishop went big with a knee bend thing that had to be out of the old-school playbook. Magdalena seemed amused at Bishop's antics but didn't tell him to rise. Instead, she smiled and ignored the kneeling agent as if he were of no consequence.

"Darby, darling. How are you?" she asked like we were old pals, and I'd been scarce. Truth be told, to her, nine months may as well have been a blink of the eye even if it had felt like decades to me.

"I'm good, Mags. How's tricks?"

Bishop took that opportunity to sputter, breaking free of his kneel to shoot to his feet. "Mags? *Mags*? Do you have a death wish, Adler? Who in their right mind calls the Knoxville vampire queen fucking Mags? Are you actually trying to die?"

I snorted and walked up to the dais to give Mags a hug. If Ingrid owed me, Magdalena owed me twice. Not only had I saved her ass, but I'd also kept her whole nest out of hot water and prevented a ghoul war to boot. I swear, the ABI could learn a thing or two from someone like me.

Mags' touch was like ice, the blood running through her undead flesh roughly the temperature of a sub-zero freezer. Young vamps were cold to the touch if they hadn't fed recently. Magdalena's was cold twenty-four-seven.

She gave me a quick squeeze and invited me to sit at her right, the chair usually reserved for honored guests.

The pair of us ignored Bishop's sputtering as he stood with his mouth agape, goggling at us like he'd never seen either of us before in his whole life.

"They could be better, honestly. I'm sure you've heard about the attack?"

I nodded. "I was in the building when it happened, but I didn't see anything. Bishop pulled me out of there before anything really went down."

Mags spared Bishop a glance before turning back to me. "My sources say it was a group of un-nested, but with what happened in January, I'm not so sure."

"I just heard about that," I replied, nodding my head to Ingrid, who sat perched at her queen's feet on the marble steps. "Was the culprit ever caught, or do they have any leads?"

Mags gave me an indelicate shrug, which didn't fit her regal appearance one bit. "Not that anyone has said," she muttered, casting a sidelong glance at Bishop. "But we've heard whispers in the community. Some of the ghouls who were there don't even remember being in Tennessee on the night in question. They had no idea how they arrived at our borders or why they were here. Not that anyone has dug too deep into those claims."

She quit the sidelong glances and outright stared at Bishop. Bishop, to his credit, was staring right back.

"I can't comment on an ongoing investigation. You know that."

Ingrid scoffed, her eyes flashing red for a moment before she calmed herself down. "What investigation? Your team, your agency has done exactly fuck all. Investigation my ass."

Bishop's face practically solidified as he met the tiny vampire's stare. "We are doing something. Just because you're too blind to see it doesn't mean we're sitting on our asses."

Ingrid rose from her perch on the steps, facing off against Bishop. "Yeah, right. All the ABI does is police people stupid enough to get caught. You know damn well that a smart enough criminal could get away with mass murder under your noses without breaking a sweat."

I thought of Tabitha and the sheer number of murders under her belt. Ingrid wasn't wrong.

"The ABI is full of corrupt thugs and shady back-alley deals," she continued, her voice getting louder and louder. "You know I'm right. You know, La Roux. Don't pretend."

Bishop's eyes flashed gold for a second before he closed them with a wince. Defeated, he turned and walked to the closest pew and took a load off. I was surprised he hadn't stormed all the way out. I couldn't say that Bishop was an ABI company man, but I was under the impression he liked what he did for a living.

I wasn't a fan of the ABI by any stretch of the imagination, but I kind of thought they were a little better than what Ingrid implied. With Bishop's refusal to defend them, it was almost as if he agreed with my tiny vampire friend.

That was not a good sign. Especially if my mother was at the helm.

"Maybe I can help?" I asked, peeling my gaze off Bishop and back to the vampire queen. Sticking my nose into things was sort of a hobby of mine. If shit was going down, I wanted to know what I was dealing with before the next attack decided to spring up in a place without an escape hatch.

Mags gave me a calculating smile. One I wasn't sure that I liked very much. "If there were anyone I'd trust outside of my nest to look into this, it would be you."

I realized way too late that Magdalena had maneuvered me into this, which wasn't exactly unsurprising when it came to the vampire queen. The last time I'd saved her bacon, she'd semi-conned me into looking into a fringe sect of the were-cats that were terrorizing parts of the city. Luckily, I'd found them quickly, realizing all too soon that it was a wild group of teenagers who hadn't even grown into their paws yet. They were just fortunate that none of them had killed anyone, or else there would have been nothing I could have done to keep the ABI out of their shit.

Magdalena was the unofficial ruler of these parts. Sure, Knoxville had were-packs all over, a few witch covens, a boatload of mage covens, and more than a few ghoul nests. But everyone looked at the vampires as the trendsetters and rule-makers. No one wanted the ABI to stick their nose in arcane shit, but the vamps?

That was a whole other ballgame.

"How many boons can one person rack up in this nest, Mags?" I asked, leveling the queen with an expression that told her I wasn't the same fresh-faced newb I'd been a year ago.

I knew where I came from now—even if I didn't like it.

Mags gave me a sly smile, one meant to cajole rather than irritate. "As many as are needed. The ABI might not like you helping people like us, but your services here do not go unnoticed. Your sense of law and order is more like a sliding scale rather than a rigid iron fist. You weigh each offender based on merit and possible threat, rather than an ancient rulebook designed to keep the arcane out of power, out of touch, and under their thumb."

There was nothing for me to do but agree with her. The ABI hurt more than they helped more often than not. I'd never been a fan, and that was before I found out my mother was the reigning bitch in charge.

"I'm not stupid," Mags continued. "I know where you've been for the past nine months. Every single arcaner from here to the moon has heard what you did.

Everyone knows that you likely saved us from the end of us all. Shiloh St. James has been telling anyone who would listen about how you kept her and the whole Knoxville coven alive. We know, Darby."

The praise felt uncomfortable, and I gave Mags a shrug. "Anyone would have done the same if they could have."

Magdalena sat forward on her throne and leveled me with an expression so fierce it took everything in me not to cower in my seat. "I know you're working for the ABI now. Truth be told, you helping us from this side goes a long way to show the people of this city that you still care about us. That they haven't changed you while you've been gone."

There was the faint thread of a threat in that statement, and I wasn't the only one who heard it. Bishop, in all his removed glory, stood from his pew.

"You have the gall to say that shit to her?" he growled, approaching the dais with a rage I'd never seen on him. "She spent nine months in prison. Nine. Being poked and prodded and tested. Biopsies and bone marrow tests, and who the fuck knows what else? All because she made a deal to keep me alive. All so the coven wouldn't be held accountable for their breach in the accord. All so her father could stay breathing." The line of his jaw might as well have been made out of granite, and if he ground his teeth any harder, he'd crack every single one of his molars.

But I couldn't look at Bishop anymore. Someone had to have told him what happened because it sure as shit would have never been me. I vaguely remembered Sarina talking about Bishop losing his shit. He'd been different since I saw him last, and it didn't seem like it was just the attack.

She told him. Dammit, Sarina.

"You think she wouldn't have endured that shit if she didn't care about this city? You think she would have just let them do those fucking tests day in and day out for almost a fucking year unless she had a damn good reason? All due respect, but fuck you very much."

Bishop marched up the dais steps as he shouldered the bag full of files and snagged my hand, pulling me from my seat. "Give me shit. Who I signed on with and the deal I made, I deserve it. She doesn't, and you won't talk to her like she owes you something. Especially when it's plain as day who owes who."

With that, he turned his back on the vampire queen, her enforcer, and the rest of the nest, who seemed to be poking their heads out of their hidey-holes. I didn't want to be on the wrong side of Magdalena, but the more Bishop's words ran through my head, the more I realized the truth in them.

Those words felt like a balm and a barb all at the same time, and I had to outright ignore the burn in my eyes that heralded tears.

Shit. I could not cry in a vampire's nest. Even with as much of an in as I had here, showing weakness was not a good idea.

I heard a faint displacement of air that signaled a vampire moving at top speed. Then Ingrid was standing in our way, the tiny enforcer barring the exit.

Greeeaaaat. That's all I needed today, to die the day I got out of prison.

Really, it was just my luck.

Bishop tucked me behind him, which was cute as hell, truth be told. Big, bad death mage was protecting the little lady like I couldn't hold my own. Well, we were in the middle of a vamp nest. There wasn't too much either of us could do if they decided it was dinnertime.

Ingrid stepped closer, her face giving nothing away as she approached. Then, she smiled.

"I guess you aren't so bad after all. Even if you are an ABI douche," she razzed Bishop, and it was all I could do not to laugh.

Ingrid's gaze landed on me, and I saw a faint trace of pity in her eyes. Of course Ingrid pitied me. She hadn't been on a losing side since Rome fell. "My queen would like to work with you on this problem, but she understands if you are overtasked. She appreciates any help you may give us."

Her formal speech was likely from Magdalena herself and was as close as I was ever going to get to an apology. I hadn't known a vamp to ever say sorry, and I knew I would be dreaming if I heard it from a queen.

"I'll do what I can, but I make no promises, okay?"

I wanted to help. I hated that the ABI building had been attacked. Hated that there were no answers and too many questions. But I had to keep the people I loved alive and out of hot water, and unfortunately, that fell to me.

The enforcer's eyes flashed red for a second before she gave me a nod and moved out of Bishop's way. He didn't waste any time and yanked me behind him as he hauled ass to the door.

"Oh, Darby?" Ingrid called once Bishop and I were nearly free.

I tugged Bishop to a stop and glanced over my shoulder. Ingrid knew something. There was no way she would stop us if her queen had given us leave. If Ingrid had info, I wanted to know about it.

"You might want to start in your own backyard. Just a hunch, but there is a damn good reason why arcaners try to stay out of Haunted Peak."

I frowned at her for a moment before facing the door once again.

What the hell did that mean?

As soon as we reached the cathedral stairs, I felt a familiar and unwelcome pull at my middle. It was as if someone had taken a hook and yanked me through a keyhole backward. Flashes of the city whizzed by my face as Bishop snatched us through the shadows. All too quickly, the world slowed down, but not before I nearly vomited on the pavement. I didn't, but it was close.

"What the fuck, Bishop? Warn a girl next time. Shit," I groaned and nearly toppled over as the world righted itself.

Fuck shadow walking or jumping or whatever the fuck he called it. I swallowed back bile and prayed I wouldn't puke.

"Aw, come on, Adler. You just walked into a vampire nest like a badass, but you can't handle a little shade jumping?"

Rather than answer him, I just flipped him off.

When I could stand up without wanting to die, I quickly recognized the park he'd spirited us off to. It was the same park where we'd sort of met. Granted, it was the same park where a body had been dumped, but I was choosing not to think about that. No, I was thinking about how it was barely a mile from my house.

Bishop had taken me home.

The darkness of this park had nearly sent me into a tailspin last year. On a night like tonight, I would fear what was crawling around in the dark. It was almost a joke how naïve I'd been. How new. There were so many things I'd been afraid of, and now my fear had been whittled down to something smaller.

The shimmering gray of specters flitted in and out of the trees. Last year, I'd have been afraid they'd come talk to me. Scared they could turn violent. Now, I wondered if they needed to move on. Were they attracted to me because I was a doorway to somewhere else like my father? Or was it something else?

My gaze drifted from the ghosts that haunted the park to Bishop. He was staring at me, too.

Shit.

Without the threat of death or the nauseating shadow bullshit—I suddenly felt supremely awkward. Just the look on his face reminded me of his big speech in the nest.

I hadn't wanted Bishop to know what I'd endured. Mostly, it was because he'd think he was responsible, and he wasn't. Sure, he'd benefitted from my incarceration, but I hadn't really done it for him.

Swallowing hard, I maneuvered around him and headed for my house. I wanted to call Sarina and make sure she got out of the building. I wanted to know what she knew. Then I wanted to sleep in my bed and eat leftovers, and maybe watch a little TV.

After that, I would dive into these stupid case files before my ax-wound of a mother came calling.

Bishop—like he'd done all night—grabbed my hand, drawing me to a stop. I didn't want to turn back to look at him, and I wouldn't have. Except Bishop pulled me again, spinning me just so, and then I was facing him. His black eyes were practically molten, the heat of them scalding me.

It seemed like so long ago that we'd flirted over tacos. So long since we hinted at a possible chance of a future together. Had that only been this morning?

But having him in my bubble, with that look on his beautiful face, was all it took for me to remember. It was all it took to bring back all my awkwardness, all my inadequacies. I took a step backward, dropping my chin to stare at my feet.

"Please don't walk away from me," he murmured, moving further into my space. I'd thought he was close before, but I was way, way wrong. His front brushed mine as his fingers found my chin and tilted it up. The heat of him filtered through my clothes as his breath tickled the skin of my lips.

How long had it been since I'd even kissed someone?

Two years? Five? Did I even still know how to kiss someone?

Then his soft lips hit mine, and it didn't matter if I'd forgotten how because Bishop sure as hell hadn't. His fingers found themselves threading into my ponytail as he took charge of the kiss, gently pulling my hair as he commanded my mouth. A flash fire of heat swept over me. It was all I could to cling to fistfuls of his shirt as his tongue tasted and explored my mouth, staking his claim so thoroughly it was as if every other kiss I'd had before him never happened.

Seriously, it was as if he'd given me a kiss lobotomy because never in the history of ever had a kiss yanked me out of my own head before. Never had I contemplated defiling a nearby picnic table in the middle of a public park. Never had I been so happy that my house was merely a few blocks away.

Breathlessly, I dragged myself back, and this time, I was the one to yank him into motion, tugging him behind me as I marched down the sidewalk toward my house.

Bishop's chuckle was low and dark, making goose bumps rise on my arms. We had a lot to talk about—I knew that—but right now, I wanted to see how fun making out on my couch would be.

At a quick clip down the street, we arrived at my

dark house in no time. The problem was that my house wasn't exactly void of people. My living room curtains were wide open, the light from my house spilling onto the lawn as a mini crowd of people made themselves at home on my couch. Sarina, my father, J, and Jimmy sat on my oversized sofa while Mariana lounged on my favorite velvet accent chair.

Groaning, I marched up the walk and through my front door, meeting this bullshit head-on. It was tough to be mad at any of them, but especially not Sarina. She'd sent Bishop to me, getting me out of the ABI building intact. If Mariana weren't just chilling in my living room for the second time today, though, everything would be roses.

"I thought I told you to stay away from him," Mariana growled, her gaze not meeting mine but staring at Bishop and my interlaced fingers. Even in my haste to get in here, I hadn't let go of his hand.

"And I thought I told you to fuck off and die. Seems like neither of us are getting what we want." My words were ballsy, but I was under no illusion that they wouldn't come without consequences. Mariana had already threatened literally every single person I held dear in my life. But that was a tougher act to turn into a reality when she'd just been attacked on her home turf.

My father snorted out a laugh and surreptitiously

scratched his nose with his middle finger. It took all the decorum I possessed not to bust up laughing right on the spot.

"Please tell me you at least saved the files you were working on," Mariana huffed as she crossed her arms over her chest.

Defensive much?

I stared at her blankly. No, "I'm glad you got out okay." No, "What took you so long to get here?" No, "This is what happened." All she gave a shit about was the files that I miraculously managed to smuggle out of the ABI building while we were under supposed fire.

A sinking feeling settled in my stomach, but I was thrilled I had the mother of all poker faces. Listening to ghosts day in and day out, you learned not to react to anything. I was a motherfucking pro.

My desire to keep what I knew to myself was only increased by the pale visage of Hildy hiding in the mouth of my hallway, out of Mariana's eye line. Hildy put a finger to his lips and shook his head.

"Files?" I asked. "What files?"

Mariana shot out of her seat. "You know damn well what files. The murder cases I was having you investigate. Where are they?"

I gave her an innocent shrug. "I don't have them."

It was true; I didn't have the files. Bishop did. But she didn't need to know that.

Mariana's eyes bled from blue to black, the inky color taking over the sclera. My solid wood coffee table went flying without her touching it, slamming into the wall before breaking to pieces. She walked through the newly open space, her black eyes piercing me to the spot.

"I know you had them, Darby," she hissed through clenched teeth. "I know you took them. Where. Are. They?"

With my hand still in Bishop's, he yanked me behind him and faced off against my mother.

"She doesn't have them," he growled, no longer the subservient agent he'd been this morning.

Her eyebrows raised in answer before she began to laugh. "I bet you've been doing that all day, haven't you? Protecting her. Don't you know by now that she doesn't need you to? Don't you know by now that she could take our lives in the blink of an eye? You stupid child."

"She doesn't have them," he repeated, refusing to move. Sure, he was telling her the truth, but I didn't want him to be on the chopping block, either.

"Why do you need them?" I asked, threading calm into my voice. De-escalation was a skill of mine, even if it likely wouldn't work here.

Mariana's black gaze moved from Bishop to me. "The

file room was raided in the attack. The record keeper was killed, and the case files burned. I've been locked out of the system. So, I'll ask again. Where are they?"

"Kevin?" I squeaked, a wave of despair hitting me square in the chest at the thought of the messy clerk. I didn't look to Mariana for confirmation, either. I cast my gaze to Sarina.

I hadn't noticed before, but Sarina was cuddling one of my pillows, and someone had placed a whole box of Kleenex in her lap. The floor at her feet was littered with used tissues. Sarina had to have known that Kevin had a crush on her, and the poor girl was beating herself up about it.

"Who gives a shit about a lowly record keeper?" Mariana growled. "Where are the fucking files?"

A flicker of spectral gray caught my eye before I heard a welcomed Irish accent.

"I think that's about enough."

The burr of Hildy's words hit the whole room like a slap. Cane in hand, his solid form glided through my living room quicker than lightning.

Mariana's spine went straight, her entire body practically frozen before she slowly turned to the sound of her father's voice. "Well, look who decided to show up. I've been calling you all day."

Hildy's face seemed to solidify even further as his expression went from irritation to something akin to rage. "I don't answer to you, daughter. I never have."

Mariana scoffed. "You made that quite clear, haven't you?"

While the pair of them faced off, Bishop and I moved farther into the room, circling the back of the couch before my living room turned into a grave talker fight night.

"Oh, because I didn't make her like you and your siblings? Because I didn't turn her into a ruthless fecking harpy like you?" Hildy shot back, the rage in his voice seeming to make his presence on this plane more and more real. "I prepared her for a different world, Mariana. One with just a little bit of compassion and thoughtfulness. If you wanted her to be a copy of you, maybe you should have raised Darby yourself rather than grasping for power."

Hildy's skull cane, with its glowing eyes, grew brighter, his rage or maybe his pull of the power in it, shining bright for all the world to see.

Mariana scoffed, a derisive snort as she gestured to his cane. "Grasping for power. That's real rich coming from you. You know they still whisper about you in the halls when they think I can't hear. About how my father commanded the armies that decimated the ghoul invasion of Ireland. About how the French shifters cower to this day when they hear your name. About how you urged armies of dead soldiers into rages, winning even after their death. And you shame me for wanting a name for my own?"

"I do when you can't see what you're doing to the world around you," Hildy protested, shaking his head.

"You put your own daughter in prison for an act that you yourself should have prevented. You punished her for a death she was owed. You threaten her family and friends, her allies, not because you worry she'll level a city or kill hundreds of people, but because she needs to learn her place in your eyes. You may have birthed her, but you're no mother, Mariana. I thought you were spoiled before, but it wasn't until today that I have been ashamed to call you my daughter."

The laugh that escaped Mariana's mouth was a thing of nightmares. "Do you honestly believe I give a shit what you think of me? Do you think I give a shit what *anyone* thinks of me? You might not realize this, but I'm trying to keep me and mine breathing. Anything after that is merely a bonus."

I wondered who her people were because she sure as hell didn't care about the agent who lost his life today. All she cared about were the records that Bishop had in his backpack.

"Tell me why you want them," I interjected, their familial standoff less important than people actually fucking dying. "You obviously think the people who broke in were after what you sent me to find, so why don't you come clean? You gave me a bullshit timeline and nothing to go on. Cough up some answers, or so help me, you will come to understand what I can actually do when I'm no longer amused."

Because something told me she didn't have the base she might have had this morning. She didn't have backup. And without a whole fucking agency at her back, Mariana didn't have shit, and she sure as hell didn't have leverage.

Not over me.

Mariana's red lips curled into a snarl, and Sarina smartly snagged the arm of both my father and Jimmy, hauling them off the couch and out of harm's way. J was already up and away, years of being on the force training enough. Then there wasn't a couch in between her and me anymore, the oversized sofa sliding into the wall, so Mariana had a clear path to me.

I didn't let Bishop pull me clear this time, either. No, I pushed him out of the way, my palms lighting up like Christmas. "If you want to do this, we can. Or you can get your shit together, stop destroying my stuff, and start talking. Either way, you aren't throwing your weight around. Not in my house. Not without consequences."

Facing off against my mother, I hadn't realized that even with heels, she wasn't nearly as tall as I was. It probably shouldn't have made me smile, but it did.

"It's your call," I taunted, practically begging her to

do one more stupid thing so I could knock her dumb ass into next week. Or the next life. I hadn't decided.

Mariana blinked once, twice, then a third time before her eyes faded from black back to their standard blue. It didn't matter the color change, the expression on her face could have lit a dumpster on fire. "You want to know what I've been trying to keep under wraps? You want all the details? Fine."

That "fine" was more gritted teeth than anything else.

But it would do.

"You have got to be shitting me," I muttered, rubbing my temples for the fifth time. My mother had to be full of shit or yanking my chain or the absolute dumbest dumb bitch to ever grace the planet. "In all your vast intelligence and covert knowledge, you had me dig in the goddamn archives when you knew someone was watching these specific files?"

I asked for clarification because Jesus, Lord in heaven she was practically begging me to kill her. Either that, or she wanted me dead for real. Given her current attitude, it was really dealer's choice.

"I told you already," she said for the third time, "I

didn't know if they were watching me or the files themselves."

"So, you used your daughter as bait?" Jimmy—who had been silent up until now—piped up.

Jimmy, J, and my father had been in the middle of planning a little welcome home party when Sarina arrived at my house with Mariana in tow. I could tell Sarina hadn't wanted my mother to follow her, but she really couldn't do a thing about it.

"Is that why you also left her to rot in prison for nine months? To throw them off your scent?" my father accused, spearing Mariana with a glare that had made better people than her wet themselves.

Mariana was in deep shit—and not just from the people in this room. She'd been working behind the scenes to try and figure out the connection between Tabitha and the Angel of Death. A link that hadn't seemed to be there at all until she'd started digging. Before I'd taken Tabitha's life, she might have had an easier time finding out what she wanted to know, but since Tabitha's soul was toast, that lead was dead and buried.

It was hard to feel bad about Tabitha—especially since I would also love to know who she was and why she wanted to raise my real father from his prison—but her life hadn't been more important than the man who raised me.

"Sounds more like penance if you ask me," I grumbled before I got up from my perch at the island. Stalking across the room, I snatched Bishop's abandoned backpack and brought it back to the group at large. "Here are your stupid files, but don't get your hopes up. It's the shittiest police work I've ever seen. The holes in the medical examiner's report alone are fucking suspect, but the lack of investigation makes me want to scream. The only thing I have to go on is a vague comment from a vamp about how arcaners stay out of Haunted Peak. Which tells me exactly dick."

I slapped the files, one by one, on the granite as the threads swirled like a tornado in my brain. This had to be an inside job, right? I mean, even if the cases weren't conducted by the same agents, there had to be something tying these deaths together.

I mean, why else would there be an attack on the ABI building just hours after I'd gotten access? Why else would someone set fire to the records room? And why wasn't there a digital back up? What was this, the '80s?

Mariana smiled at me, a genuine one this time and not the snide curl to the lips that made me want to punch her right in her face. "Haunted Peak was built on the bones of arcaners. It's why I chose it for us to live in the first place. And it's not about what's here," she said. "It's about what's missing. Mr. Hanson? Care to see if you can show us?"

We all turned to Jimmy as a blush rose to his hairline. Self-consciously, he tucked a strand of hair behind his ear to reveal the lone visible feature that identified him as an elf. It was common knowledge—at least to me—that the Fae could see through glamours and around obfuscation spells. But J was out of the Jimmy loop, his eyes going wide at the sight of Jimmy's pointed ears.

"I'll see what I can do," he mumbled, his embarrassment at being outed as an elf nearly killing me. I could practically taste it on my tongue, and it made me want to punch my mother even more than I had before, and I hadn't thought that was possible.

I shot her a glare, but she was focused on Jimmy, my gentle giant of a friend, who in no way should be pulled into this mess.

"There seems to be something with the photos," he murmured, his voice barely above a whisper as he inspected the first case file, singling out a photo and bringing it closer to his face. "This isn't the real picture. Is this the ABI's version of classifying? Slapping a badly constructed obfuscation charm on the file and calling it a day? My nine-year-old cousin could break this in her sleep."

Mariana gave my tall friend a little smirk. "I'm sure she could, but elf magic is a whole other practice, as you well know. Tell me what you see, Mr. Hanson."

Jimmy raised his head and stared at my mother. "I don't know what you want me to say. What you see on the photo isn't what is actually there." He rose both hands and snapped his fingers. A tiny burst of gold sparks lit with the sound. "Look for yourself."

Mariana snatched the photograph from the island, and her face went white.

"I fucking knew it," she mumbled before slapping the photograph back down on the counter in front of me. The picture was mostly the victim's body. Ferris Laramie was being inspected at the crime scene by a small female medical examiner, her dark curls causing bile to rise in my throat.

Tabitha.

She had been the one to inspect the body of a man who likely couldn't have thrown himself down a ravine. The same Tabitha who convinced hundreds of people to murder for her here in Haunted Peak. The same Tabitha that had been trying to raise my father from his prison.

Now it wasn't just a guess that these deaths were connected. It was for damn certain.

I passed the photo to Bishop, who was trying not to launch himself across the island and slap the shit out of my mother. If he held any tighter to my counter, he'd break the stone off, and I'd really be pissed.

Furniture could be replaced. Counters were expensive.

"How long did you know?" He spat the question through gritted teeth. "How long did you suspect she'd infiltrated our ranks? How long did you sit on this shit and wait for it to blow up? How many people are dead because you did nothing?"

Bishop may have started his questions in a low, menacing growl, but by the time he'd ended them, he was practically shouting.

"You sent me down here to keep an eye on Darby. To make sure she didn't try to raise him herself when she knew nothing of him. You sent me here when you knew she wasn't the one you were looking for because these deaths had happened long before... I swear to everything holy, you will go in front of the tribunal. Headquarters is going to know exactly what you've done."

Mariana threw her head back and laughed. "You silly, stupid boy. Who do you think I've been hiding from?"

Bishop looked like she'd socked him in the gut. Hell, I probably looked about the same. Mariana's lone statement about how she was hiding from headquarters implied a whole host of shit I was not prepared to think about.

And I wasn't working for them by choice.

Bishop had alluded to a deal he'd made when we were in the Dubois nest. A deal he regretted.

Shit.

Sarina, in all her oracle wisdom, latched onto Bishop's arm before he could do something supremely stupid. I knew very little about my own powers and probably less than nothing about Mariana's. Who knew what she could hit him with if he wasn't careful? Plus, who knew what she would do to him, or who she had in her back pocket?

Bishop's jaw was in danger of breaking under the strain of his gritted teeth.

"You stupid, selfish cow," he fumed, practically vibrating with rage. "How long have you known?"

The repeated question did nothing to move Mariana. Instead, she sniffed, inspecting her manicure before plopping back onto my favorite chair. "A while. Well, almost as long as I've had the job. I have a feeling that's why I've progressed so fast. Keeping your enemies close and all that."

That didn't make much sense to me. "If you're hiding from them, why tip your hand? I mean, if you don't want them to know you're on to them, why wave a red fucking flag in front of a bull?"

Mariana gave me a scathing glare like I was some simpleton that needed shit explained in crayon. "I put you away for damn near a year. They were supposed to think we were on the outs. If you went poking around, they would assume I was out of the loop. It's why I slipped a few cases in that weren't exactly what I was looking for. How in the hell was I supposed to know he'd immediately send someone to burn the place down?"

Stunned, all I could do was blink at her. And then it wasn't Bishop that needed to be held back.

It was me.

I'd nearly reached Mariana before Bishop's arm banded around my middle, and my father had put himself in between me and my quarry who had smartly vacated her chair in favor of making herself a moving target.

"You left me in there to rot for nine months because you were throwing someone off your scent? Do you have any fucking idea what they did to me, you bitch?"

I was amazed the windows didn't rattle with as loud as I was screaming. But did she care? Based on Mariana's stony expression, she absolutely did not. Had I really ever come from her? Even my birth father who had been imprisoned for years treated me better than this woman.

I wanted to slap her. Hell, I wanted to set her on fire or launch her into the sun or tie a cinderblock to her ankle and watch her thrash in the ocean.

And Bishop's iron hold was pissing me off. I didn't want to hurt him, but if he didn't let me go, I was gonna.

Biopsies and tests and everything else. I'd have nightmares about needles until the end of time all because she wanted plausible deniability. All because she wanted to throw some nameless, faceless boogeyman off her trail.

"Of course I knew," she snapped back. "Who do you think ordered the tests? It had to look authentic."

She really should have kept her mouth shut on that one, because one second I was struggling against Bishop's hold, and the next he and my father were ass over tea kettle on the floor and I had Mariana in my sights.

But did I kill her? Did I choke the life out of her? Did I snag the Glock I kept in a tucked-away gun safe under my favorite chair?

No, I did not.

Instead, I did the sensible, rational, non-homicidal thing.

I punched her right in the face.

Cocking my arm back, the move was as telegraphed as a punch could get. Too bad Mariana wasn't what I'd call a fighter. She seemed almost surprised I'd accost someone like her, the shock on her face almost as good as the crunching impact of my fist against her jaw.

Also?

She was a fucking wimp. One little baby punch and she was out like a light, crumpling to the floor like a sack of potatoes.

My father—who was still on the ground—stared at

his former wife in awe before he snorted out a guffaw. Killian Adler wasn't a fan of violence, and he'd never, ever raise his hand to anyone. But seeing his ex on the floor? He had zero problems with that.

Sarina plopped onto the chair Mariana had vacated and stared at Mariana, shaking her head.

"I told you she would make you eat your words one day," she chided her unconscious boss. "You should have listened to me."

I couldn't help it. I snorted out a laugh. Only Mariana would ignore a psychic.

"Oracle," Sarina corrected, rolling her eyes.

"We talked about this," Bishop groused, scolding Sarina on reading thoughts without permission. Really, I needed some mental wards or something.

"Yeah, yeah," she replied, waving off Bishop's words. "Wards are all well and good until some jerk infiltrates your office and kills one of your friends. You think you want wards on everyone just so you can get a moment's peace, and then poof! You remember why you hate them." She sat back hard in the chair, sadness etched on her face.

"You know what happened isn't your fault," Bishop murmured, dropping down in a squat by Sarina's seat. "We were all caught off guard. Just because you see a lot doesn't mean you're a god. You can't put that kind of pressure on yourself."

Sarina shook her head as she wiped a tear from her eye. "It's my literal job. I'm supposed to keep an eye on threats. I'm supposed to find people who can't be found. What good am I if I can't do that?" She sniffed and Jimmy handed her a box of tissues. "What am I even doing here? I mean, I knew something was up, but had I known she was hiding from the brass, there was no way I'd have signed on. I thought I was doing some good in the world, and after the attack in Ascension, after today, how am I supposed to get ready for work every morning and look at myself in the mirror?"

I tried to put myself in her shoes. Had there ever been a time I couldn't trust my captain? Was there ever a time when I thought he was doing wrong or I didn't trust him to lead me?

I couldn't say I had ever had the misfortune of not trusting my leadership. Just the thought felt awful. But maybe if I were in her position, I would stay like she had. Maybe I would try to do as much good as I could while fighting for change.

That's all anyone could do, right?

Sarina sniffed again before loudly blowing her nose into another tissue. "You're right," she said, reading my thoughts once again. After the day she had, I really didn't mind. Kevin had been a sweetheart. A really good guy who was killed for no good reason. Sarina deserved a freebie pass on my thoughts just this once. "I can't get out of my contract, but I can do good while I'm here."

My gaze fell to my mother, her slack body still crumpled at my feet. She couldn't answer a single question I had if she was unconscious. But maybe I didn't need her. I knew someone who knew Tabitha long before she came to Haunted Peak.

I was going to have to call Shiloh St. James.

"You punched the Knoxville ABI Director in the face?" Shiloh asked like she couldn't see Mariana still passed the fuck out on my living room floor.

I wondered if I should be concerned that Mariana was still passed out after that punch to the face, but decided that if she was still breathing, it really wasn't my problem.

She'd heal. Probably.

"Yep," I answered, popping the "P" with an unrepentant grin. "She deserved it."

Shiloh in all her Amazon-tall glory had come alone to my house, leaving her coven goons behind. The last time we'd met, she'd had her whole coven with her as they'd tried to stop an evil bitch from hell from raising my birth father from his prison. They were... unsuccessful to say the least. Shi and I had been friends for years before that, but the fact that she'd known about the secrets buried in my own backyard put a solid strain on our relationship.

"And she's your mother?" Shiloh asked, still staring at Mariana like she'd jump up any second and take us all to jail.

"Uh-huh. She's a real peach, too, but I'm sure you knew that already."

Shiloh snorted before shooting me a grin. "I always knew I liked you, Adler. So, you've got me here, said it was an emergency. Please don't tell me you need me to hide a body because there is owing someone, and then there's *owing* someone."

"Oh, please. If I wanted to bury her in my backyard, you'd be the first one here with a shovel and you know it. But no, it doesn't have anything to do with her."

I crossed the room and pulled the photograph Jimmy revealed to us from the file. Jimmy had been hard at work removing the glamours from all the photographs and reports, but it was slow-going. Passing the picture to Shiloh, I asked, "See anyone you recognize?"

It took Shi less than a second to spot Tabitha crouching over the victim. "You've got to be shitting me.

What the hell is she doing there? How old is this photo?"

"It's from 1997. When was Tabitha in the Knoxville coven? Do you have any idea what she was doing here before you kicked her out?"

"That's not her name—or at least that's not the name she gave us. I want to say she was with us from 1990 on through the early 2000s, but I wasn't in charge back then."

I wanted to laugh, but I was pretty sure it would be considered bad form. The previous leader had been killed by mutinous members of her own coven who'd tried to hide their usurping tendencies behind some heavy curses. That crime scene had not been pretty.

"Do you know anything about her? Who she hung around, what she was doing in the coven? Anything you could tell us would be helpful," Bishop said, his politeness at full force since Shiloh seemed to hate him. A lot of the arcaners I ran with hated the ABI. Their reasons seemed to be good ones, but I wondered if they hated the ABI because of a few rather than the many.

Shiloh shook her head, a frown marring her beautiful face. "I-I can't think of anything." She shook her head harder like she was trying to clear it. "Why can't I think of anything?" She stood from her seat, fear etched on her face as she began to pace around the room. "I knew her. I swear I knew her. Her name was… it was… Why can't I think of anything?" she repeated, the distress in her voice making it sound shrill.

Out of all of us, it was Jimmy who sprang into action. His big body was up from his seat and across the room in an instant, and he had his giant arms around her as he cooed in her ear, "Shh, it's okay. I know what's going on here, and you're going to be okay."

Just like the case files that hadn't made any sense, and the deaths we couldn't explain, someone had been monkeying around with the truth, and I didn't like it one bit.

Shiloh had been spelled to forget, and we were at another dead end.

"Okay, Obi Wan," I eyed Jimmy, "share with the class."

Jimmy picked his big blond head up off his cuddle with Shiloh, a slight frown marring his beauty.

Gah! Has he always been that pretty?

"It's odd magic," he replied. "Old. Older than Fae magic. I haven't seen it in ages. But it's concentrated on her head, so it has to be a memory working." He guided Shiloh to sit on my disheveled couch. "I don't know how to undo it, so I figure it shouldn't be messed with. The web of it is too messy."

It was J who piped up then, wonder coloring his words. "You can see it? The magic, I mean?"

It was something like interest on his face, which I

hadn't seen since the great Johnny Ruxby love affair in college. J was about as good at picking partners as I was —AKA, we were fucking terrible at it. But I had a good feeling about Jimmy.

Jimmy nodded. "Most of my kind can see magic. It's how I knew Darby wasn't human the moment I met her."

He flicked his hair back over his pointed ears and settled beside Shiloh on the couch, his blush so high on his cheeks, he may as well have been a tomato.

But J wasn't blushing. Oh, no. His focus was now laser-locked on Jimmy, and I could practically see the thoughts swimming in his brain. I just hoped he pulled his head out of his ass.

And soon.

But a hope for a possible love match wasn't going to help me figure out who Tabitha had been while in the Knoxville coven, or who she was working for before her untimely death. I was tempted to kick something in frustration but decided against it. Instead, I rummaged through my takeout menu drawer and prayed someone was open late. With Hildy so close, there was a definite drain on me, and after so long without that feeling, I realized I was in no way used to it.

I needed calories. And caffeine. And sleep.

I also needed to figure out who had the fucking gall

to mind-wipe the Knoxville coven leader, what to do with my mother—who was still passed out on my living room floor—and what takeout place was open this late. I was trying to decide between the all-night Indian place or making the trek to *Si Señor's* when J, Jimmy, and my father's phone all rang at once.

Given the day we'd all had, it was tough not to let my stomach drop at the sound.

There were only two reasons all three phones would go off at the same time. One: our precinct had been attacked just like the ABI had. Unlikely, but I wasn't ruling it out. Or two—and far more probable: there was a body.

At J's "Yeah, Cap," I knew which one it was. As I listened to the other end of the line, my mood did not improve, however, it did do a teensy uptick when J handed me the phone.

"Hello?" I answered, trying not to be nervous.

"If it isn't my favorite detective. The FBI steal your phone, kid? You can't call anyone?" The words were scolding, but full of a love so big, I wanted to burst. I had to wonder what Mariana had told him last year when I was up to my neck in shit. It wasn't like the ABI gave me an opportunity to clean up my life before they threw me in jail.

I gave Uncle Dave—AKA, Cap—a nervous chuckle.

"You know the deal. Gotta let people miss me sometimes. I hear you've got a body."

"I hear you're back in town. Want to help an old man out and take a look-see?" Cap asked, giving me exactly what I wanted. I couldn't say why, but I did not want J going out there without me.

"Well, I guess. If you really want me to," I joked before getting serious. "I missed you guys. You know that, right?"

"You know you have a place here as long as you want it, right? Any time you want to flip off those FBI bastards, you come on back. I've got your desk ready for you."

Cap might as well have punched me in the gut. It was all I could do not to start crying on the phone. I mean, Cap wouldn't care, but I hadn't cried in front of him since I was fifteen and the first boy I'd ever liked had broken my heart.

"Quit being mushy," I croaked. "I'm giving you back to J before you unman yourself, okay?"

Cap sniffed, a sure sign he was either already crying or about to start. "Yeah, yeah. Love you, kid."

"Love you, too," I replied before handing the phone off to J. And if I needed a Kleenex, well, then I was allowed.

Nine. Months.

Almost a year had flown by without anyone to talk to. Without Dad or Dave or J. My circle had always been small, but it was a good one. I couldn't imagine going back to a life where I missed out on all my people every day.

I wanted my life back. I wanted the life I had before all this shit started. I wanted my job and my small group of friends. Hell, I'd pay to keep my secrets from the general public and be a town pariah again.

And as daunting and horrible as it was that there was a body to be investigated, I was still excited to get back out there. Man, how fucked up was I?

Once I got myself under control, I rejoined the buzzing group milling around my half-demolished living room. The whole room was wired, and I didn't have a good feeling as to why.

"What?"

J pinched his brow like he was trying to stave off a headache, which only happened when shit was not adding up.

"The body is at Deadman's Gap," he said, like it was supposed to mean something, and then it clicked.

"Ferris Laramie," I muttered, and J nodded his head.

Who the hell could forget a name that preposterous? J had been staring at the same damn files with me for the last little bit, and a man being pitched off the side of a mountain into a ravine was kind of a big deal. I'd probably never get the sight of Tabitha kneeling over his corpse out of my brain.

And Deadman's Gap wasn't exactly a happy place. There had been plenty of stories over the years about people committing suicide in that particular pass.

"What are the odds some hiker just fell, and it has nothing to do with the case I'm working on?" I asked, a tiny sliver of hope still in my heart. That could totally happen, right? A hiker or hunter or someone slipped and fell, and it was just a coincidence.

Bishop snorted out a chuckle. "Gee, Adler, I had no idea you were such an optimist. Anybody mind if we tag along?"

I didn't mind one bit. But I was technically on the outside. J had been doing this without me for almost a year. Maybe he had a new process. Maybe he did things different. I looked to my best friend.

J, in all his wisdom, rolled his eyes at me. "Go get your badge and your gear. You're running point. It'll give the boys a heart attack." He rubbed his hands together, an evil glint to his smile. "If this shit day and this shit case had any silver lining, it's that. Sal has been getting lax as fuck without you around. I can't wait."

Back to work *and* I got to torture Sal? I couldn't wait.

I just needed to figure out what to do with my unconscious mother first.

"What the fuck do you think you're doing?" I barked as I watched Sal Whitestone trample all over what could have been preservable footprints in the sandy shore.

Sal was inside the yellow tape, a strawberry frosted donut in his hand as he plodded about in the dark. At my shout, he froze and slowly turned to the sound of my voice like he was trying to pinpoint a rattling snake. He visibly swallowed his bite of donut before schooling his expression as best he could.

J wasn't exaggerating even a little, and these fucks were about to learn today.

"D-Darby Adler. I didn't know you were back," he replied, ignoring my question altogether.

"You're standing on evidence, Sal," I growled through clenched teeth, my plot to exact revenge already swimming in my head. "Do you remember what happened the last time you stepped on evidence? Hmm?"

Sal's already-pale face went white. "You taped sardines to the bottom of all my desk drawers and filled my whole car with shaving cream."

"Not that you could prove it," I replied, smiling in a way that could never be construed as friendly.

"Not that I could prove it," he parroted. "But it's not my fault this time. It's dark and the lights aren't set up and…"

I held up a hand. "That's enough. What's the rule?"

Sal frowned at me like he was going to start yelling about how he had seniority and I was some upstart who was the town freak. Before he could open his mouth, I stopped him.

"The rule is to not go past the yellow tape until the lead detective gets here. Especially if it's dark. *Especially* if you can't see anything. And why is that?"

"Because if I can't see anything, then I could be destroying evidence, and evidence is how we keep guilty men behind bars," Sal replied on a monotone voice, the answer falling off his tongue by rote since I'd drilled that shit into his head.

"Exactly." I slapped Sal's shoulder. "This is your freebie since I've been gone so long. The next one will cost you. Now get behind the tape and try and find me the person who called this in," I called over my shoulder, but I turned back, approaching him once again. "Please. You're a hell of a lot better at talking to people than me," I offered, throwing him a bone. Sal had been on the force since before I was born and probably should have retired a decade ago. He knew everything there was to know about Haunted Peak—the human version of it, anyway.

Sal blushed before shuddering a little. "I'd like that better, anyway. This place gives me the creeps. Full of old ghosts," he mumbled gratefully, turning away to leave the scene. I had to wonder if he was a little more receptive than I gave him credit for.

Because Sal wasn't wrong.

Places like this I tried to avoid at all costs. Cemeteries. Monuments. Suicide cliffs. There was this bridge out in the boonies people talked about where people went to die. Places like that were filled to the brim with ghosts. People who couldn't or wouldn't move on. People who begged for their final rest only to get stuck here waiting. My only solace was that my father wasn't here. I'd put Hildy in charge of watching Dad and making sure he stayed firmly planted in the land of the living. It was a small comfort, but I'd take it.

This tiny little ravine was riddled with glowing see-through specters. Some milled about, seemingly unaware that the gully was packed with living humans. Others were staring at the humans as if they had forgotten what the living looked like. Others just appeared angry.

I wasn't a fan of an angry ghost. Especially an angry ghost that was staring right at me.

"I know that guy," Bishop hissed in my ear and I jumped, breaking eye contact with Ragey McRagerton to stare at him.

"What?"

"The dead guy," Bishop clarified, not helping in the least. "I know him."

I pulled him closer to hiss in his ear, "You're going to have to be more specific. This place is crawling with ghosts, and one of them looks like he's about two seconds away from going full-blown phantom."

I broke away from Bishop and found J. "Get everyone out of here. Code Boo."

J's eyes widened, and he let out a whistle that hurt my ears. Granted, it had the desired effect, and techs and detectives and everyone else all popped their heads up. "Clear the area. I repeat, clear the area. Possible methane leak detected."

A gas leak was a bullshit reason to clear everyone out, but it was tried and true. I just had to hope this ghost held off until everyone was clear.

If only I was that lucky.

"Code Boo?" Bishop snickered in my ear as he tagged my elbow in his large hand. How he'd gotten to me so quickly was a mystery since I couldn't peel my eyes from the dead man across the gully. You know, the one that seemed so close to losing it.

"Adler?"

"Yeah," I whispered back, not taking my gaze off the no-longer-living man sporting a crisp suit and tie and a lanyard hanging around his neck. He looked vaguely familiar, but I couldn't place him. If Bishop knew who he was, then he had to be with the ABI, right?

"What's a Code Boo?" he asked, his breath tickling my ear. I could hear the smile in it. If he only knew...

"It's a feral ghost in the vicinity who may become a

poltergeist and harm people. She wouldn't call it unless there was an actual threat, and she's trying very hard not to spook the spook," Sarina answered for me, which I appreciated. I had a feeling if I moved, the man was going to turn. "Help me clear these people out. We don't have a lot of time."

It had been a long time since we'd had a poltergeist on hand, and even longer since I had to deal with one so pissed off. Calming specters was a specialty of mine, but I couldn't exactly do that with a crowd of people watching.

I'd rather not trade in my prison stay for a psych one.

Plus, I had no idea what could happen now that I actually had juice. It wasn't like before when I *didn't* light up like a Christmas tree. Now, I wasn't so sure.

When the majority of people were out of earshot, I made the likely stupid decision to approach the specter. Of course, it was just my luck that this guy not only knew who I was, but he also seemed to be pissed as hell at me.

Goodie.

I picked my way through the gully, trying not to get my boots wet. Not that it mattered. I had a feeling I'd be running from this guy before the evening was over.

"You," the man hissed when I was in earshot, and it was all I could do not to beat feet back where there were people and lights and some modicum of safety. It was an illusion of safety, but whatever.

"You know me?" I asked, pitching my voice in a soft, conciliatory tone that I hoped spoke to him. It did not.

The man approached, doing that thing that ghosts did where they glide superfast and scare the shit out of you. Getting right in my face, it was all I could do not to scream my head off and take off running. "You're the reason I'm dead, so yeah, I fucking well know you."

Super. He knew he was dead and blamed me and knew all the ghost tricks to frighten the fuck out of me. We were getting off to a great start.

I did my best to calm my heart rate—and my brain— and ask the important questions. Too bad my voice still trembled. That wasn't winning me any points.

"Why am I the reason you're dead? Can you tell me anything about the person who killed you? Anything at all would be helpful." If he knew what was going on, I would sure as hell capitalize on it. There was nothing worse than an angry ghost who had no idea why he was angry.

But my trembling tone and questions seemed to make him even madder. *"Why am I the reason you're dead?"* he repeated my question in a snotty voice, screwing up his face in derision. "Take a wild fucking guess, Adler."

It was tough not to get back into old habits of

absolutely hating talking to ghosts at night. Hadn't I been all big and bad a few hours ago in the park? So much for that level of confidence.

But this guy really did know me, or my name at least. Sure, he looked familiar, but I had no idea who the fuck he was. As someone who did their absolute best *not* to get people killed, his implication pissed me off. I growled under my breath and tried to tamp down the flare of rage that lit me up like a brush fire. Well, it was better than fear.

"Why don't you spell it the fuck out? In case you were out of the loop, I have no idea who you even are. Moreover, I have no idea why out of all the people in the world, I would be responsible for your fucking death. So, pretty please, get your head out of your spectral ass and give me some goddamn info before I deport your sorry self to the hereafter and find out myself."

Were my hands glowing like lanterns in the middle of this gorge with possible witnesses? Maybe. But my threat seemed to do the trick. Ghost boy was still mad as hell, but he relaxed some, backing out of my space.

"I work—*I worked*—at the ABI. I was an analyst assigned under the director."

Okay, that was useful info, but it still didn't tell me dick. But I let him continue without prompting.

Sometimes specters just needed to talk out what they could remember.

"I was one of the agents assigned with bringing you in," he elaborated, which told me where I knew him, but not what he was doing dead in a giant ditch. "When the building was breached, it was like the people who dealt with your case—the ones working under the director— were all targeted. It was as if they knew where we were in the building. They came straight for us."

That opened up a pit of dread in my stomach for sure. "It was un-nested vamps, right?"

The man nodded, his anger fading a little. "Kenzari told us to get out, that it wasn't safe, but the director told us to stay put. Then she left us there to die. She killed us. She fucking killed us."

I covered my mouth so I wouldn't start raging right here in this stupid fucking ravine. How many deaths were on Mariana's hands? How long had she known Tabitha was killing people before she acted? And if she was trying to protect "me and mine," as she said, then why leave these poor agents to die while she fucked off to safety?

None of this made any sense.

"If you were killed at the ABI building, you must have seen who killed you, right?" I prompted, hoping to have something to go on. I seriously doubted the vamps who stormed the building knew what they were doing, or if they did, I suspected their reasoning was a lie. Whoever was pulling the strings was working extremely hard to stay hidden.

Man, did I miss the days when killers were easier to find.

"Un-nesteds attacked, but the man who killed me was no vamp," the dead agent said. "It was a white-haired man in a suit. Never seen him before. Looked young, but you could tell he wasn't, you know?"

I nodded, massaging my temples. Most arcaners quit aging young. Vamps stopped when they were turned like Ingrid. Ghouls could be born or turned, and the turned ones could outlast the born ones by a couple of centuries, but like vamps, that could be anywhere from a few hundred or thousands of years depending on who turned them. Most natural-born arcaners aged at different rates. Witches had the most human lifespans at about two hundred years, but that was if they didn't dabble in the hard stuff. Shifters lasted longer at about five hundred years or so. Mages could last forever if they didn't piss off the wrong person, but most of them failed in that endeavor.

So, this guy could be a hundred years old or a couple of thousand, with any age in between. Meaning his thousand-yard stare meant precisely fuck all, except he probably had more power than I did.

"The vamps called him 'X' when they weren't calling him master. The Knoxville nest might be calling them un-nesteds, but they serve someone, and it isn't Magdalena Dubois."

With that, I let out a groan. I was going to have to talk to Mags again, and I was pissed at her. Perfect. But what would she be able to tell me? I mean, Shiloh had been mind-wiped about Tabitha, agents had been killed and dumped, my mother had left people behind, and what? How was all this shit connected? I picked a clear spot on the ground and parked my ass there. Why would someone dump this man where another person had died?

I swear my life was peaches and fucking roses before my mother walked back into it.

Hating that I was coming up with more questions than answers, I wallowed in my tired, pissy question-laden glory until I spied a dark pair of boots in my narrow field of vision. Bishop lowered himself into a squat so we were eye to eye. The concern etched into his expression was doing very odd things to my middle.

I kind of wished we could rewind the day a few hours. Maybe leave the park or run away to literally anywhere else. For the first time since I'd been in this life, I wondered if I could hang it all up. Take a break. Go on vacation somewhere where no one knew me and live in peace for a little while.

I doubted such a thing was possible. Stuff like that just wasn't in the cards for me, now was it?

"I don't like that you're doing this by yourself," Bishop began, and then it dawned on me that Bishop wasn't just concerned. He was pissed. Somehow in all my wallowing, I'd missed the line to his shoulders and jaw. I'd missed his rigid posture and stony expression.

"I do not like that you're dealing with poltergeists by yourself or putting yourself in harm's way. I hate that I just got put on crowd control duty, but moreover? I loathe that you could have been hurt."

I couldn't help it. I laughed. A hysterical giggle that signaled that I was ten steps past losing my mind—if I'd ever had it to begin with. I almost fell over I was laughing so hard. The exhaustion and fear and sheer confusion at this shit day landed on my shoulders all at once.

Wiping at my tears, I finally replied, though my answer was filled with giggles. "I don't like it much either, but nothing bad happened. Sometimes specters just need a friendly ear. Why people—living or dead— think I'm the ear they want to bend, I have no idea, but that's my lot in life. Now, do you know the agent that was dumped here?"

Bishop nodded, and I spied a peek of sadness glinting in his eyes before he hid it behind a stoic mask. "Scott Greyson. I worked with him."

At his somber tone, I didn't know if I had the heart to tell him that Scott wasn't the only one that had died at the ABI building. Likely all the people he knew—all the people he worked with day in and day out—were probably gone.

"La Roux?" Greyson whispered, and it made me jump. I'd forgotten he was here—a feat I thought totally impossible since he'd been a tiptoe away from going into a full-blown ghostly temper tantrum.

"You made it out. Man, that's good news. I thought..." Greyson trailed off, seeming to get upset when Bishop made no move toward his voice.

"He can't hear you, Scott. But I can, and I'll translate if you want me to."

Scott seemed shocked for a second, like the realization that his life was over had finally hit him. Sure, he'd *known* before, but now it was real. I'd seen it too many times before, the aching knowledge that no one wanted.

The ghost swallowed before giving me a hesitant nod.

"Scott was in the ABI building when it was attacked by vamps. They weren't with the Dubois coven but unnesteds. He was killed along with many of his colleagues in a targeted move that seemed geared toward agents that worked for the director. According to Scott, they were singled out specifically."

I paused before adding in a little tidbit that might mean fireworks but needed to be said regardless.

"She left them there," I whispered, unable to leave the absolute horror out of my voice. "She told them to stay put while she escaped and left them there to die."

And that was around about the time that Bishop La Roux lost his fucking mind.

Have you ever seen a death mage go full monkey shit? Yeah, me neither.

Not until right then, and I had to say, it was the most frightening fucking thing I'd seen since Tabitha's soul clawed its way out of her body.

I sure was glad we were in a secluded area and the place had been cleared out, because if the humans could see this shit, the arcane cat would be out of the bag.

If I'd thought Bishop was pissed before, I was sorely mistaken. I'd never seen someone lose it while also going fluid before, but there I was. When Bishop finally lost his grip on his anger, he was a sinuous beast of black and purple swirls of magic, his magic wafting from his shirt and hair as it leaked out of his body. I did not want to be Mariana right then—or ever, really—but definitely not when Bishop had snapped.

Even Greyson—who had lost his life just hours before—didn't want to be anywhere near Bishop now that he'd lost his leash.

"She swore to me that no one would be left behind. She swore," he growled, a strange golden light illuminating his irises.

"Bishop?"

I couldn't believe how small my voice was. It wasn't like I feared him, because I didn't. I sure as hell worried what consequences he'd suffer if he went off half-cocked.

Bishop whipped his head to me, the golden light in his eyes growing brighter, becoming beacons in the darkness. "She deserves their wrath, Darby. She deserves to be where they are. She deserves—"

"Stop it right now, La Roux," Sarina barked, startling me since she seemed to have popped out of nowhere.

My relief came quickly at her presence. A crazed ghost I could deal with. A gonzo death mage? Not so much.

"What you're thinking will only cause more death and destruction. You cannot fix this by stealing a life, and you cannot raise those who have left this world. You got lucky when Darby took your place in prison. She had a bargaining chip. You don't. Calm down before I make you."

Bishop's rage was palpable—I could almost taste it on my tongue. But Sarina's words rang true. He didn't have a bargaining chip, and whatever he was planning—as horrific and likely justified as it was—was going to get him killed.

"She earned this," he growled through clenched teeth. "She deserves to die."

Sarina huffed out a bitter laugh. "When has anyone ever gotten what they deserved in this world? Do we deserve to work for this agency if they treat their people as disposable? Do I deserve to honor my contract even though they have broken their end? Do you deserve the deal you made for a wrong that was never yours?" She shook her head, her expression pitying. "But those are the deals we made and contracts we signed and the hand we've been dealt. A reckoning is coming for Mariana O'Shea. Just you wait."

I couldn't say why out of all the horrors Sarina had uttered, the realization that my mother had reclaimed her O'Shea surname hit the hardest. It was small—a tiny betrayal I couldn't really describe—but it was that last grain of sand on an already-overflowing scale.

Tears pricked at my eyes at the sheer gall, at the fucking audacity of it all. There had never been a time where death did not seem like a large thing. That people's lives didn't seem precious. That the lives I was responsible for as a police officer and detective weren't vitally important to me.

How fucking could she?

And as bad as Mariana was, she still wasn't the murderer I was looking for. She might have left this man to die in her stead, but she wasn't the person who killed him. She might have left him as bait, but someone else had taken it.

And it made me so fucking mad that she wasn't the actual bad guy in this scenario that I wanted to scream. I sincerely hoped there was a special place in hell for people like Mariana.

But I probably wasn't that lucky.

"Darby?" Bishop called.

Slowly, I managed to look up at him. He was no longer in danger of raging out all over the ravine, his coal-black eyes back to normal, his magic back under wraps. A springtime breeze fluttered through the air, cooling the wetness on my cheeks.

I dashed at the idiotic tears and sniffed. My sorrow was stupid, and it didn't serve anything except to prove that my mother was dead to me in all the ways she could be. She was not my mother, and I'd never think of her as someone I shared any ties with whatsoever.

I swallowed, cleared my throat, and stomped my emotions back down into the pit of my stomach. They belonged there, anyway. What I did not do was answer him, because what was there to say? She changed her fucking name? How in all the atrocities she'd committed in just the last twelve hours did that even rank?

Instead, I met Scott's gaze. "I want to inspect your body and the scene for clues. I know you were dumped here, but I would still like to check. Would that be okay?"

Scott blinked at me, seemingly stunned I would ask. Unless the entire scene was cleared, did I ever ask, but if the owner of the body was there and I could, I tried to be respectful.

"Y-yeah, I suppose that would be okay. But... are you okay?"

I couldn't recall a time when a ghost—especially not a fresh one—asked me that.

"No, I am not, but I can get the man who killed you, and that'll help."

Scott's face was the picture of concern. Bishop and Sarina probably appeared the same, but I didn't check. No, I pulled the Nitrile gloves from my bag and got to work.

. . .

Leave it to Jimmy to get all the photographs while I was in the middle of a drama. J and Jimmy had processed three quarters of the scene by the time I'd hauled myself over the stream to the dump site. Either J or Jimmy had marked off the scene with tape, first an inner square that encompassed thirty feet around the still-untouched body. Then there was an outer square that spanned about sixty feet around.

It was just like riding a bike. All of my processes came back to me like I hadn't just been in prison for damn near a year. Before I entered the outside square, I donned my booties and lit my flashlight. The brightness of it almost hurt my eyes as I searched the ground for anything amiss.

The damp ground was a map of footprints, and I mentally cursed Sal and whoever else was dumb enough to trod all over a scene like a herd of buffalo. As carefully as I could, I minced around the prints, sticking to the tufts of grass that wouldn't disturb the silty sand. Three hops later, I was to the inner square, and I had to fight the bile rising in my throat at the sight of Scott's body.

There was nothing nice about Scott Greyson's death. Not in the manner in which his body had been dumped, not in the way his life was taken—nothing. Even though I knew he was not killed in this ravine, there were pieces of him scattered about the inner square like scavengers had gotten a piece of him.

Except... the pieces of Scott were whole, displayed with a purpose, and with the stench of enough magic to make any animal within a mile want to run for cover. Each piece was laid out methodically and meticulously, on purpose and with intent. Whoever put him in this ravine not only wanted me to find it, but they also wanted to taunt me.

What was with arcaners and mutilated corpses? One would think they had better things to do with the rest of forever, but alas, it seemed they did not.

Foregoing my usual headphones, I crossed the tape, picking my way through evidence. I swear, if I could have figured out a way to hover over the body, I would have.

There was very little left on the inside of Scott Greyson. His heart, lungs, stomach, and liver had all been removed, placed in an almost halo arching over his head. But it was the damage done to his face that made me want to puke like a rookie. There weren't words for what was done to him, and trying to think of them made me want to cry.

"Please tell me this was done to you after..." I muttered to myself.

"Yeah," Scott answered, nearly making me jump a mile. "It was the throat. He cut it."

I knelt, careful not to put my knees in the sand, and inspected Scott's neck. Well, what little there was of it. If his throat had been cut, the wound was efficiently masked by well... not being there anymore. I tried to recall what Scott had said about his killer.

"Didn't you say he had white hair? Do you remember what he looked like? Any other features?"

Because we sure as hell weren't going to get anything from the knife patterns on his neck, that was for damn sure.

"It was weird," he replied. "It was almost like he didn't have a face. When I looked at him, all his features were gone. Like a no-see spell. And it didn't break when I died, either. All I know is that he had white hair and wore a suit."

"Skin tone? Tall, short, skinny, fat? Did he walk with a limp or have any visible tattoos?"

Scott's face screwed up like he was trying to remember but the picture in his mind was illuding him. It didn't seem like memory magic exactly, more like a glamour powerful enough to go past the grave.

"Pale skin, but not undead pallor. He was tall, maybe six feet or so. No limp or tattoos. Trim build. Definitely male. Other than that, I'm sorry. I know that isn't much to go on."

It really wasn't. But something niggled at me.

"You said they—the un-nesteds—called him 'X,' right? So, he's a white-haired, old-as-shit, Caucasian arcaner with a name likely starting with X. How many of those are walking around Tennessee, right?" And how many had an army of vampires at their disposal?

I was really going to have to talk to Magdalena. Or maybe Ingrid would do. Ingrid would know all the gossip, wouldn't she?

"Did you say the vamps called him X?" Bishop asked from the edge of the inner square. "You're sure?"

Looking to Scott, I gauged his expression. Scott seemed to think about it, the agent in him wanting to help as best he could. "Yeah, I'm positive. It stuck out."

I relayed the message and Bishop's face turned to stone.

"Fuck," Bishop muttered before reaching for his phone. "I gotta make a call. Don't go anywhere, Adler. You hear me?"

His tone did not speak of happy tidings. What else was there to do but agree?

"I'm kinda in the middle of something here. I won't be going anywhere anytime soon."

A trill of unease hit me square in the chest, and I

thought my unease was at peak levels already. Trying to focus, I studied the wound at Scott's throat. Knowing vamps were involved, I could see the wound patterns for what they were—a disguise. Everything about this was fake. Scott's wounds weren't the ritual of a serial killer or for a spell working.

There weren't sigils carved in his skin or in the ground. Not unless his organs were covering them, but I doubted it.

It was all fake. A show.

We were back at square one all over again and it was pissing me the fuck off.

I struggled to keep myself on task, trying to catalogue all the visible injuries, the position of the body, the wounds that were more a macabre window dressing than anything else. But my unease grew. Bit by bit, minute by minute, until I could feel the disturbance on the air. Scott and I might have been working together to solve his murder, but I knew the second his attention shifted.

Looking up, I followed his sight line to the edge of the ravine and saw the blonde woman who was standing at the edge of my crime scene like she had any right to be there.

I knew it the moment Scott turned. It was that little pop of pressure that told of a poltergeist's power. Usually, the fresher the dead, the least amount of power a ghost had.

Unless the death had been beyond traumatic.

Unless the body had been desecrated.

Unless the ghost knew about the arcane world.

So even though Scott Greyson was brand spanking new to the flip side of life, even though he should have been no more powerful than a newborn baby, the whole ground moved when he turned. One second he was talking, even chuckling a little, and the next I was knocked off my feet as the change took him.

There was a damn good reason why a Code Boo was a legit thing. Because there was no such thing as a safe poltergeist and trying to banish one was about as easy as riding an angry bull or playing chicken with an ostrich.

I found myself tangled in yellow police tape as Scott launched himself at Mariana, sorely tempted to leave her to her own devices. She was a grave talker. It wasn't like she was helpless.

And the truth was that she'd earned his wrath. She earned every single bit of his anger, every bit of his punishment.

But the problem with leaving an enraged ghost to their own devices was that it wasn't just their quarry that they hurt. They hurt any and everyone who was in their way, anyone near enough to them, anyone unlucky enough to even resemble a vague representation of their catalyst. So soon, it wouldn't just be Mariana who was on the receiving end of Scott's punishment. It would quickly turn from Mariana to any blonde woman to just any woman. Then it would go to any human, and then...

It wouldn't stop. Ever.

Somehow, I found my feet, racing after the ghost as fast as my feet would take me. Which wasn't very far. Almost immediately I realized what I'd missed in the initial burst of adrenaline. There was something wrong with my right arm. Either it wasn't in the right spot or it was broken. Either way, I was down an arm all while running on rocky terrain after an enraged specter.

Scott's howls of fury echoed through the canyon, the power in them making rocks float up off the ground, the wind whip, and the stream surge. Trees swayed so hard they nearly broke at the bases, and all the while the land pitched and rocked as if we were at sea. I couldn't make out what he was saying, but it didn't matter if the words were in my language or not. It didn't matter if they made sense at all.

Nothing mattered except to contain this spirit before it harmed anyone. I didn't know if we were held accountable for what we did while we were ghosts, but I didn't want this man to earn punishment if he didn't deserve it in life.

"Stop, Scott," I yelled, but my words were swallowed whole by the howling wind.

Down a useful arm, and without much backup, I raced after him as fast as I could, skidding to a stop in the damn sand when Mariana sailed through the air in my direction. She should have stayed where I put her instead of getting in the middle of this. Was my back porch so terrible? No. It was a damn sight more comfortable than kissing dirt, that was for damn sure. Before she could land on me, I dove out of the way, the impact of my meet with the ground rocketing through me.

And because my luck was just that terrible, when Scott followed his rightful quarry, he found me instead.

The man with the chiseled jaw and impeccable suit was long gone. In his place was a thing of nightmares representing his body in the real world. His chest cavity yawned wide as he raced for me, the wide-open maw of his body, the mutilation of his face, everything making me want to scream my head off and run away.

A regular ghost was bad enough. This was worse. So, so much worse.

Struggling to stand, I felt the icy touch of Scott's ghostly hands wrapping themselves around my upper arms. He lifted me, his fingers burning me they were so cold, his now-distorted maw in my face as he screeched at me.

And then just like Mariana, I was airborne.

This time, my landing was not a happy one—not that the one prior to it was in any way awesome. No, this time I landed in the stream, the rocks digging in my skin in some places and breaking it in others. And this time, Scott followed me, his mangled ghostly face in mine as he let out an unholy shriek. He shoved at me, dunking my head under the water.

I didn't want to take Scott—not like this—but my options were all gone.

It wasn't until I decided to take him did that part of

myself seem to unlock. The last time I did this, I had no idea what I was doing. This was no different. I still didn't know what I was doing, and after almost a year with no practice, I was back where I started.

My lungs burned as Scott's soul was called to me. The anger in him resisted a little, but it was no match for the siren song of the beyond. He was in pain here, and the call spoke of peace, of rest. I had no idea what it really was, but I hoped it wasn't bad. Still—even after so much time—I didn't know where the souls went or why I could take them.

I just knew I was a portal of some kind. Just like my real father.

But when Scott fell into me, it wasn't like the others. I couldn't see from the outside of his life, a casual observer witnessing his pain and anguish.

No, now I was in it.

Kenzari was in my face, grabbing me by the shoulders and guiding me to a portal exit. I couldn't hear anything over the siren, but that was sort of the idea. If vamps had breached the ABI, then the siren was supposed to disguise our footsteps so we could make it to safety. It was the Protocol C plan in the handbook. Phillips had already masked the servers so no one could gather intel, but it was my job to make sure the paperwork on our desks went into the incinerator.

But Kenzari wasn't having it.

"Screw protocol, Greyson. Get the fuck out of here before it's too late," she ordered, her gaze getting that far-off quality that she always got when she was looking ahead. "I expect you to be right behind me. Do not make me ask twice."

I liked Kenzari. I liked her a hell of a lot better than our boss. But who really liked the director? No one with a brain in their head.

As far as I was concerned, our boss was the reason I hadn't seen my bed in a week and likely why we were being breached in the first place. I mean, why else would we be attacked unless it was because of her?

With who her daughter was, who her family was, with what she'd had us doing…

This was just like January. Just like the ghouls. Just like that shifter who was killing randoms. It was connected. I knew it was connected. But I couldn't prove it. Someone had control, influence, and a boatload of power.

And we'd gotten too close.

"I'm coming. Get to a portal. I'll be right behind you," I told her as I dumped an armful of papers in the incinerator. "I have one more desk to do, and then I'm done."

"No, Greyson. Now," she said, her fingers digging into my flesh so hard it hurt.

"O-Okay," I stuttered and got moving. She led me to the transportation room, and I was right behind her, I swear... But I remembered the photograph in my desk drawer. The one of Cora. It was the last thing I had of her. I had to go back for it.

Kenzari was at the portal and through it before I turned around, racing back to my desk. I'd snagged the picture and was about to go back when the director stomped through. Following her were about ten of my coworkers.

"Get everything in the incinerator. No trails, no nothing. I don't want to see one shred of intel on this floor, or I swear to everything holy, you won't live to see tomorrow."

The director didn't make idle threats, and if the breach was for intel alone, we needed to follow protocol to the letter.

But a minute later, the director was gone, and we were surrounded in a room with no exits. The breach countermeasures meant we couldn't get out of this room, couldn't do anything but wait to die.

And die we did.

Scott's soul was sad. He'd been born into a mage family with little power, little money, and few prospects. He'd married a human woman for love, not realizing that even with his limited abilities, he still had a very long mage life ahead of him. Cora had died the century prior in childbirth, their first and only child dying with her.

Nowadays, Cora would have thrived. She'd had big ideas and even bigger plans. Scott missed her every day.

He didn't mind leaving this earth, and he was excited to go where she was if such a thing were possible.

Absorbing his soul was bittersweet, the pain of his death hitting me everywhere as if I were experiencing it through his memories. But his love for his wife was a balm, too. It was a relief and a misery.

My lungs screamed at me, my entire body ached, my brain was a fuzzy mess, and I couldn't remember why I couldn't breathe. Two pairs of hands latched onto my arms and then sweet air kissed my lungs.

Breath whooshed through my airways for the first time in who knew how long, and all I could do was cough and sputter and try to ignore the blistering pain in my whole body. I had hoped that sending Scott on to his rest would be a relief, or at the very least a way to gain *some* knowledge, but I knew no more now than I did before and probably had some burned brain cells to show for it.

But darkness yanked at my heels, pulling me down. I should rest, right? Resting was good.

"Darby Adler, I swear to all that is holy, if you die, I will figure out how to yank your ass from the Underworld and make you pay," a gruff male voice said.

I assumed it was Bishop, but everything was dark, and I couldn't make out who it came from.

Why was everything so dark?

Did Scott hurt anyone else? Was everyone okay?

"Is she breathing?" J asked, a mild panic in his tone. "Why isn't she breathing?"

Why was he panicking? I was fine, wasn't I?

But the darkness didn't lift, and the world didn't get clearer, and the sounds drifted away...

A man's voice whispered in my ear, a muffled consonant of a sound, and then it felt like I was being shoved off a cliff with no safety net underneath me. Light burst everywhere: inside my brain, outside my body, there was brightness so sharp, it almost hurt to look at it.

Time to wake up, kid. There's no resting yet. Not for a while.

It was another man's voice—one I was sure I'd heard before. I *knew* it, but grasping at it just like everything else was so hard.

My eyes flashed open, and even though it felt like my whole body was being ripped apart, I dragged in another breath. A coughing fit racked me, the shake to my ribs an agony I hadn't yet experienced before now.

Man, I could have done without that.

"Do we need a bus?" J asked, and I wanted to ask

166 | ANNIE ANDERSON

who needed an ambulance, but I had a sneaking suspicion it was me.

"Maybe, but I think I know where we can go that might be better suited for her. The last thing we need is her lighting up like a damn supernova in the middle of a hospital. Good thing you guys claimed there was a gas leak."

Fuzzily, I focused on Bishop's face.

"Did anyone get hurt?" I croaked, my voice sounding like broken glass.

Bishop knelt down and lifted me in his arms. "Just you, sweetheart. Just you."

He cradled me there for a moment, the warmth of his body seeping into me. I hurt everywhere, but that one little bit of comfort almost lulled me to sleep.

By the time Bishop danced in the shadows, I was dead to the world.

17

There were few things worse than waking up with a hangover and knowing you didn't even get to drink. Sunlight streamed in from a nearby window bright enough to sear my eyeballs, lighting my brain on fire. I reached for anything that would cover my head. A pillow, the covers, a shirt, anything, but all I found was a warm chest that most definitely did not have a shirt on it.

I sat straight up, the action alone being one of the top things I regretted in my life. It was only slightly behind losing my virginity to Tommy Salisbury my senior year of high school, and that one time I thought wearing white pants the day after I thought my period was over was a good idea.

Everything hurt. Everything. My arms, my legs, my skin, my brain. Hell, my internal organs felt like someone was taking a blowtorch to them, and it probably wasn't even nine in the morning.

"Someone kill me," I rasped, cradling my head in my hands. Anything to get the sun to stop roasting my eyeballs.

"Been there, done that. I would prefer it if you were among the living, if you don't mind. I can't see the dead, remember?"

Then I remembered that there was a person, sans shirt, in my bed, and now I knew who it was. I peeked through my fingers to see a bare-chested Bishop laying right next to me. He rested his head on his hands, his arms cocked up in the way men did when they knew they had a killer torso and wanted to show it off.

Was that pose even comfortable? I couldn't recall the last time I'd laid down that way. It seemed like a really good way to make your arms fall asleep.

Tearing my gaze from tan abs and a set of pecs I could totally rest my head on, I scanned the room. Yep, it was definitely my house, my bed, and he was most certainly laying on top of my covers.

"No offense, because I'm seriously enjoying the view here, but why are you in my bed without your shirt on?

Also, why do I feel like I've been hit by a truck? Moreover, is there coffee? Or Ibuprofen? Or food?"

I was trying to be funny, but Bishop didn't smile. Instead, he sat up and leaned toward me. His face was a little haggard, his stubble reaching toward beard territory. He looked like he hadn't slept, maybe all night, and I didn't know why.

"I'm without a shirt because you bled on mine, and I didn't want to stain your bedding. You feel like you've been hit by a truck because you went toe-to-toe with a poltergeist and nearly lost. And there are meds, breakfast, and the rest waiting for you in the living room. But I swear, Darby, you have to slow down. I know you think you can do it all, and maybe you can. I've never met a woman as strong as you. But not only did you stop breathing last night, your heart stopped as well. That ghost damn near drowned you. And that was after he threw you around like a rag doll and nearly pummeled you to death."

My brain was slow to respond. Mostly because last night was so far past hazy it wasn't funny. I vaguely remembered the mangled body of Scott Greyson, but much past that was a blur.

"So basically, what you're saying is, you're making me coffee and breakfast, and I'm supposed to sit down and let you wait on me? Because I hate to break it to you, Bishop, but I won't be the one arguing with you."

If I went ten rounds with a ghost last night, and he wanted to make me breakfast afterward, then I was pretty much in heaven. Well, as soon as my body quit yelling at me.

Bishop narrowed his eyes at me like I was pulling his leg. "You aren't going to fight me on this?"

I snorted. "No, Bishop, I won't be fighting you on this. Mostly because I can't fight shit right now. I don't even know if I can walk."

I hefted my legs over the side of the bed and tried to stand. In answer, the room decided it was time to turn into a tilt-a-whirl right about the moment I stood up, and I dumped my ass right back down on the bed.

"Well, that answers that question," I muttered, holding onto the covers for dear life.

By the time I could open my eyes without wanting to toss my cookies, Bishop was kneeling at my feet. "How about you pretend your legs don't work and I'm your transportation for the day. At least until we can get you fixed up."

Again, I wasn't going to argue. I gave him a small nod, one that wouldn't make the room be mean to me, and he picked me up as if I weighed nothing. My head was not a fan, and I clung to Bishop shoulders as if I were being hefted off the face of the earth.

What the hell happened last night?

Bishop weaved through my house like he owned it, gently depositing me on my couch like he'd been here a hundred times before. As quick as a whip, my legs were covered in one of my throws, and I had a steaming cup of coffee in my hands. There was a splash of cream and a scoop of sugar, and I had to wonder if figuring out my food preferences was a superpower of his or if he used his resident oracle for intel.

After my tenth sip of the life-giving brew, I started asking questions.

"Is everyone okay?" I frowned, trying to recall the events of the night but turning up with nothing. "I don't really remember what happened."

Bishop rose an eyebrow at me as he turned my gas stove on. A shirtless man was making me breakfast in my kitchen. Did I really die in that damn ravine, or was I dreaming? The hiss of eggs hitting a frying pan made my stomach lurch with hunger, but I managed to stay in my seat and sip coffee like I was told.

"Yeah, no one but you and Mariana got hurt, and she healed up just fine. Greyson only wanted her, I think, and you either looked too much like her that he couldn't tell you apart, or..." He trailed off, shaking his head.

"You sure you're feeling okay? I kind of thought you would remember."

"It's fuzzy. I remember his body, that's for sure. But I'm positive it would have taken a lobotomy to scrub that from my brain. After that..." I shook my head. This time it didn't make me want to hurl. Progress.

"So I take it you missed Ingrid coming by to help with the healing process, then?"

I snorted in my coffee. "Um, no. I think I would remember that. Ingrid Dubois came to my house?"

Was that my voice sounding so scandalized? Maybe, but Ingrid was Ingrid. There were things as the enforcer of the Dubois coven that other vamps just didn't do. Making house calls was one of them. Not that I understood why she would come to my rescue— especially for healing.

I must have looked extremely confused because Bishop chuckled as he plated a pair of fried eggs and began buttering toast.

"You really haven't made use of the boon she owes you, have you? As an FYI, vampire saliva has clotting properties. You were torn up from Greyson tossing you all over that ravine. With you glowing like a Roman candle, I couldn't exactly take you to a hospital. Ingrid offered her services."

It took about three seconds for my mind to process

the image of Ingrid licking me for my coffee to almost come up. "Please don't tell me—"

Bishop's eyes popped wide. "No. There was zero tongue action in this house at any time last night." He shuddered from head to toe, his face going green. "Absolutely not. There is a salivary duct in a vampire's mouth. We used—or rather she—used a syringe and extracted the necessary amount, put it on your wounds, no stitches required."

My heart rate dialed down about a zillion notches, and an aftershock of a shudder rocked through me.

"That's good. Umm, for future reference, can I just bleed to death next time? Would that work for everyone?" I was only half-joking.

Bishop narrowed his eyes at me. "How about we just stop going head-to-head with poltergeists? How'd that be?"

He used the royal "we," but he meant me. A part of me wondered what would have happened if I hadn't made Hildy follow my father to watch over him. Would he have helped? Would I accidentally absorb him? That's what I had to have done to Greyson, right? Flickers of memories flashed in my brain. A picture of a woman, my mother's face telling him to stay, the white-haired man with no face as Greyson was killed.

A plate filled my field of vision, and I dove for it,

snatching it out of Bishop's hands before he could blink. The buttery toast and an egg were gone before he sat down with his own plate.

"How do you always know what food I want?" I asked after a couple of swallows. Bishop had given me four pieces of toast, six eggs, eight rashers of bacon, four sausage links, and several slices of tomato. It was a virtual cornucopia of all the best breakfast foods.

"I had help. Sarina says hi, by the way. She, Cooper, and the director are cleaning up the crime scene mess this morning. A good thing you two have the Code Boo shit worked out already. Blaming the light on a methane explosion came in handy."

I tried to remember a light in the ravine, but my memory still had some mighty big gaps. I carefully munched on bacon and flipped through what little I remembered. "I don't remember there being a light. I do remember seeing a bunch of darkness, though, but I'm pretty sure that was the back of my own eyelids."

"It was right around the time J and I started giving you chest compressions, so you might have skipped that bit. I have to say, you sure know how to show a guy a good time. Poltergeist brawls, mutilated corpses, family fistfights. You're just a bundle of giggles, Adler."

I knew he was joking, but he wasn't wrong. It seemed like more and more that this was my life. This is what happened. My life was fistfights and corpses. It was brawls with ghosts and interrogations and asking vamps for favors.

My life was a damn mess.

Instead of replying, I picked up my coffee mug and took a sip to hide my face. This was why I didn't date. Why I hadn't had a boyfriend since college. Last night—while hairier than was the norm—was what my life was made of. How the hell was I supposed to date in the middle of this shit?

Bishop gently squeezed my calf over the blanket. "I was kidding, Darby. Mostly. The 'you not breathing bit' wasn't my kind of good time, but I'd rather spend a fucked-up night with you than a boring one with anyone else."

"Are you flirting with me, Bishop?" Had it really only been a day since the last time I asked him that?

Bishop stole my plate from my lap and plucked the cup from my fingers. Then he leaned over me, caging my body with his. "Yeah, Adler. I'm flirting with you. Is it working?"

I gave him a slight nod, and that was all it took to make him drop his lips to mine. His kiss was gentle, like I was a fragile piece of glass and he really, really didn't want to break me. He tasted of fresh coffee and bacon, and it was a hell of a taste. I wanted more, but my body was just not up for it. He seemed to sense this, his mouth gentling further on mine.

He broke the kiss, muttering, "Good," against my lips before my plate was back on my lap and my cup was in my hand.

I hadn't even put down my fork.

18

"Please tell me you're joking," J said before turning to Bishop and Sarina. "She's joking, right?"

There was a blonde woman at my door, and I was under no illusion as to who it was. All three of them were barring Mariana's entry to my house, and I couldn't blame them. Scott had attacked her for a damn good reason. The fact that I took the brunt of it only pissed them all off.

My father was sitting at my feet, squeezing a hand over my toes that were still under my blanket. He appeared haggard after learning the events of last night. Compounded with the knowledge that I'd almost died, the grooves of his face had only deepened. Hildy had made good on his promise to keep him alive, and that was all I really cared about, anyway.

"No, I'm not joking. I need to speak to Darby. If you don't move, I'll get less polite about it, though."

Mariana was pushing her luck. As the day progressed, snippets of what had transpired started coming back to me. The way she'd just shown up at the ravine. Some of the images I'd gleaned from Scott, the darkness. She'd left them there to die. That part stuck out.

"Unless you're coming in here with a damn good apology and some fucking answers, you can stay outside," I called, my back to the door. I couldn't even look at her. How could she leave them like that?

"Why else would I be here?" Mariana snapped, not actually answering my demand.

"To cause problems, to get under my skin, to exert your will to move me into a position I don't want to be in. To make me miserable because you fucking can," I volleyed back, rage coursing through me as the truth of each of those statements rang true.

Mariana growled but didn't force herself into my home, which was a teensy point in her favor. "You need to know the truth, and until you know that you're going to be in danger. Can't you just listen to me? Five minutes and I'll be gone."

Sure she would.

"Five minutes is all you get," I hissed, finally turning to look at her. "After that, Hildy gets you. After what you've done, he's been aching to talk to you."

The ghost in question was hanging out on my porch. He'd taken one look at me, saw how little I was healing, and lost his fucking mind. And that was before Bishop made me tell him what really happened. Mariana was living on borrowed time.

Mariana visibly gulped before her spine went ramrod straight again. J reluctantly stepped aside, but he didn't appear happy about it. Bishop and Sarina did not, so Mariana was stuck three feet into my living room and looking through the gap in their shoulders.

"That's far enough," Bishop barked when Mariana tried to side-step him. When she opened her mouth to protest, he held up a hand. "Unless you performed chest compressions last night, you don't get a say in this. She doesn't want you here, and I'm making sure you don't overstay your welcome."

Mariana snarled at him but quit trying to get farther into my house. Huffing, she crossed her arms but did not continue.

"Tick tock," I muttered, righting myself in my seat, so I didn't have to look at her.

"It wasn't Azrael who killed his children," she

blurted, and I whipped back around to gape at her. Never, not once, had she said my father's name. But the Angel of Death wasn't an unknown figure, even to humans. Some called him Thanatos, some called him The Pale Rider, but I didn't know for sure what he called himself.

My ribs protested my sudden movement, and I unsuccessfully tried to hide my groan. "Guys, let her in enough that I don't have to twist."

If I sounded like I'd just run a marathon, then whatever.

They let her in further, and she perched on the edge of my newly restored coffee table that Shiloh managed to fix for me. I kind of hoped it would snap apart under her, but that was just me being petty.

"I'm listening," I snapped once I caught my breath. This healing shit was for the birds.

Mariana appeared a little paler than usual, her red-painted lips standing out in her colorless face like a beacon. She chewed on her bottom lip for a second before nodding to herself. "Azrael wasn't killing his children. The ones who died were either in a war amongst themselves, or they were unaware and being killed for sport."

The story she'd told me—the official story, it seemed —was that the Angel of Death decided he didn't want the children he'd made and decided death was better for them. He began killing them one by one until it became too tedious, and he switched to eradicating them in droves. Apparently, when a man could live forever, he could also bed a shit-ton of women. When the ABI caught wind of his filicide, they'd devised a plan to bury him.

I could only blink at her for a solid minute. "You're telling me you buried his ass under a fucking mountain with a damn lake on top to keep him down, and you knew he was innocent?"

I knew Mariana was low, but I didn't think she was that low.

She shook her head. "I didn't find out until after. I tried to keep my digging small, but nothing ever added up to me. So I kept at it, chipping away bit by bit until I got it mostly figured out. Honestly, it wasn't until that idiot Tabitha raised him, did I really put everything together. The bloodthirsty thing he'd been painted as would never have let you live. He sure as hell would never have handed over Tabitha so you could bring Killian back. Once I heard your story, I knew everything I'd been told was a lie."

A nasty expression crossed her face before she hid it behind her stoic mask. "You know, I thought I was protecting you." She chuckled, searching the ceiling with her gaze so she didn't have to look me in the face. "I thought I'd been duped by this awe-inspiring being. That the time we spent together was a lie."

A single tear slid down her cheek, but she still didn't look at me. "And now I find out that I have betrayed him in the worst way—not only by burying him in the dark but by destroying his memory. And you still aren't protected. Isn't that a kick to the face?"

If this was her attempt to make me feel bad for her, she'd really picked the wrong girl.

"If you think his children were killing amongst themselves, you obviously think someone in your chain of command is involved?" I offered, plucking the meat of the issue out of the emotional bullshit. Did I think Mariana had a heart buried deep in there? Maybe, but the state of it was not my problem.

"I have a couple of contenders, yes."

"So I have—or had—a boatload of siblings who decided what? Murder was better than family dinners? Why would they kill each other?"

Mariana gave me a chuckle as she wiped at her damp face with the back of her hand. "The throne, Darby. They want Azrael's throne."

The Angel of Death had a throne? That made no sense. These people hadn't read the lore, or if they had, they hadn't used their context clues. The ABI prison might have been lax about a lot of shit, but their library was top-notch. I'd read everything I could about the Angel of Death, Thanatos, and every other death god in the known histories. None of them had happy lives, and none of them had a throne. Death work was just that: work.

"Who in their right mind would want his job? Even tangentially, this job sucks great big monkey balls. A ton of power or not, knowing the lifespan of everyone, knowing where souls are, feeling them drain you all the damn time, feeling their deaths on the way out. Yeah, you can keep that shit. It's bad enough just seeing ghosts every-fucking-where." I shuddered, the memory of Greyson's death hitting me like a one-two punch to the face.

I felt everyone's eyes on me, and the awkwardness set in. "What?"

Mariana's gaze was especially sharp as she answered, "Now it makes sense. Azrael was supposed to have an heir. The story was that he killed each of his children to prevent his heir from taking the throne. But what if the real killer was weeding out Azrael's children? What if he was trying to find the heir? What if there are only certain children who can succeed him?"

"Meaning?" I prompted, not liking where this was going at all.

"Meaning, not all of his kids could take his place—only some of them. Ones gifted with Azrael's power. I saw those arcaners—the ones they said he killed. None of them had even a whisp of the power that rolls off you. No wonder Hildy kept you practically starved. You would have stuck out like a sore thumb."

My chuckle was bitter, but I said nothing. What had Hildy told me? I could be seen from space.

Fuck.

And the only reason I hadn't noticed before now was because I was either under power-dampening prison wards, in my home that had been locked down tighter than Fort Knox, or in the middle of the ABI building…

That was attacked while I was there.

"Fuck," I groaned, covering my face with my hands. Tears were swimming in my eyes as I thought about the agents who died because I was there. Because I hadn't put it together.

No. I hadn't been the one who had them stay. I hadn't been the one who left important information out. I wasn't the one who was responsible here.

"You let those agents stay in that building knowing that they were looking for me. Didn't you?" I accused, horror washing over me. If I could have slapped her, I would have.

Mariana didn't appear repentant. Hell, I would have

taken a little guilt. Something. Instead, her face was a blank mask of indifference. I swore to everything I found holy that if she shrugged, I was going to come off this couch and fucking kill her.

"Your time is up," I whispered, wishing for the ability to kick her out of my house myself. "Unless you have more to share, I don't want to see you again. Do you understand?"

"You can't—"

"I can. I haven't killed anyone that didn't deserve to be killed. Can you say the same?"

Mariana shoved to her feet, staring down at me like she had the upper hand. She didn't.

"Do you have any idea the rage a specter can feel when they've been taken before their time?" I asked. I doubted she knew. If she just saw them as power sources, there was no way she'd actually talked to one. No way she'd tried to help them. She had no fucking idea. "How about a whole team of them? If you thought Greyson was a problem, you'd better get your affairs in order. I have a feeling you'll be dealing with a few more. How many agents did you send to their slaughter again?"

All it would take was a little whisper of a word from Hildy, and she was beyond screwed. Karma really was a vengeful bitch sometimes. I really liked that about her.

"It was better them than you," she insisted. "They meant nothing, but you... You could change everything."

Mariana still didn't get it.

"I don't want to change everything. I don't want to take a throne that isn't mine. I don't want anything, except to make sure the world keeps turning and bad guys get caught. If you don't understand that, then I can't make you, but if you knew me at all..." I trailed off, shaking my head.

I couldn't make her understand basic decency.

I couldn't force her to think about other people before herself.

I couldn't make her give a shit.

And that was the problem.

"Get out. Don't come back," I hissed through clenched teeth. I really hoped this time she'd listen. I wasn't going to be whatever vision of me she had in her head. And I wasn't going to save her ass.

"You'll see, Darby. I promise, you'll understand soon enough."

Mariana left in a huff of a woman bound and determined to make dealing with her a major pain in the ass. It was like she wanted to be thrown out of my house, like she wanted to make everything purposely difficult. I'd never met a woman so insistent on making me hate her.

It figured that she was my mother.

The silence that stretched on after her departure was a physical weight in the room. I was trying very hard not to feel guilty, but I wasn't doing a very good job of placing the blame where it damn well belonged.

It was bad enough my mother out and out admitted to being a soulless she-beast, but even with all the information she'd given us, I still didn't know who was behind it all. The ABI was vast, and I didn't exactly have good intel since the place had been breached.

I could ask a certain someone, but I didn't know how. All the plans in my head just ended with me blowing up.

"What are you planning?" my father asked, the wariness in his tone surprising me. I didn't know why it would surprise me. The man knew me better than almost anyone except for J.

"Nothing."

"Oh, man," J muttered. "I know that look. That look is the reason I spent the back half of the summer of my junior year repainting old man Duxbury's barn."

I scoffed. "Exactly zero people told you to start a bonfire in his hayloft, J. You did that shit to yourself."

"It was an accident," he hissed back. "You said I should use my telescope in a high spot. How was I supposed to know the lanterns would explode and set the whole damn place on fire?"

"Not. The. Point. I have an idea, but I don't know if I can do it. Not without help, anyway."

"Ya want to talk to Azrael, don't ya?" Hildy grumbled, sitting as far from me as he could and still be in earshot. It was weird seeing him in color, and I had to wonder how much power he was using to keep his form. Well, that and how in the hell did he just know these things? This was the first time I'd heard Hildy say my birth father's name, and it freaked me out a little.

I knew Hildy was in the loop on all things death-related, but it was still weird.

"I don't know. Out of all of us, he would know what went down back then, wouldn't he? And if he still absorbs souls even being where he is, then he might know things we don't. I know it's only been a day, but he might have more than we do. Maybe the spells that hid the killer's face from me might not work on him. He might have...*something*."

"That has to be the worst plan I've ever heard of, and you've come up with some fucking whoppers in your day," J announced. As if he hadn't come up with just as many in his lifetime.

"You got a better one? I'm listening if you have one."

No one said anything, and I stared at each of them in turn.

"I think you should go," Jimmy murmured from his perch at my island, and I nearly jumped at the sound of his voice.

I had completely forgotten the giant man was there. Damn Fae magic.

"You seem to have a connection to the man—*deity, whatever*—he might speak to you."

"The bigger problem is actually talking to him. How in the hell am I supposed to do that?"

"With what everyone has said, I think he went back to his prison on his own. I don't think he's being held there. I think he's choosing to stay."

Jimmy's suggestion had merit, but I wouldn't know until I got there, and it was the getting there that was the problem. I hadn't managed to get off this couch yet. How the fuck was I supposed to go up the mountain?

"Might need to make a pit stop at a cemetery or two on your way, lass. That specter did a number on ya."

I swallowed down bile. As far as I knew, I was safer here in my house than I would be traipsing around cemeteries on my way to go talk to the Angel of Death.

"Come on," Sarina said, offering me her hand. "Let's get you dressed."

Getting dressed while injured was the fucking worst. I hadn't had so much as a broken bone since I hit puberty, so broken ribs, healing wounds, and a boatload of bruises on top of a near drowning was not exactly in my wheelhouse. I was a whiney, pitiful mess as I longed for sweatpants and a blankie.

Whose idea was this? Oh, right. Mine.

I could have kicked myself. I probably would have if it wouldn't make me hurt from head to toe.

Dressed in jeans, a Ramones T-shirt, and Chucks, I prayed I wouldn't need to draw a weapon of any kind because just the thought of putting on my holster made me want to cry.

Sarina was busy stuffing clothes and weapons in a small duffle bag she'd pulled from my closet.

"For when you heal and can dress by yourself," she said, and managed to wedge my vest in there, too.

"Thanks." Really, I was ridiculous. Putting my bra on alone had been a chore of epic proportions. "Do you think this'll work? Talking to Azrael, I mean?"

Sarina straightened and got that far-off quality to her gaze that meant she was trying to see what would happen next. "I don't know," she muttered, frowning. "Seeing his line isn't the easiest. You are fuzzy but he is a big blur of possibilities. I think there is just too much death tied to the both of you. It's tough to see past that."

It wasn't exactly the comfort that I was looking for, but I appreciated her honesty.

"Thanks," she said, and I remembered all too quickly that Sarina could read my mind.

I winced at the thought of what she'd gleaned from me.

"No, really," she assured me. "Some people don't like when I can't answer them. But you—even if you don't like it, you appreciate it. It's nice."

It was tough to be thanked for being a decent person, and I wondered who had hurt her and if they paid for it.

No, Sarina. Don't answer that. Just let me wonder, okay?

"Okay," she replied, smiling.

Our first pit stop was dropping my father off at the office. The last thing I needed was to watch him get hurt again. I really couldn't handle it. Of course, that earned a ten-minute lecture on keeping my own ass out of the fire, to which I nodded and smiled and assured him I would be on my best behavior.

I was lying my ass off, and I think he knew it.

Still, I told him I loved him, gave him a hug even though it hurt, and waved goodbye. Then when he was out of earshot, I begged Bishop to ward his office with everything he had. Zip in, zip out. I couldn't spare Hildy this time, and the worry was going to kill me.

Our second order of business was stopping by the oldest cemetery in town. I chose this place—rather than the one closest to my house—because I wanted the souls that really wanted to leave. The thought of absorbing a soul with actual unfinished business made my heart hurt something awful.

After the way it had already been bruised, it deserved a break.

Haunted Peak Memorial Cemetery was in the historic district of town and held graves older than dirt. The oldest one in residence was interred in 1523. Most of the headstone had been rubbed off and the ghost was long gone, so I—along with the rest of the town—had no idea who it belonged to. Some said it was a Vatican priest. Some said it was an early settler. But if I was looking for old graves, this was the place.

Bishop helped me perch on one of the stone benches. This particular bench was under a weeping willow that mostly hid me from prying eyes. It didn't really matter. No one came to this part of town.

Even in broad daylight, this little piece of Haunted Peak was a ghost town. Set back from the town proper, the historic district was a forgotten memory, a place for buildings to crumble and cemeteries to fall into disrepair. The bench I was sitting on had a spiderweb of cracks in it, the stone on its last leg.

It was proof positive that Southerners only remembered the histories they wanted to and forgot the ones they didn't.

There weren't a bevy of souls left in a place like this. Many had moved on, hopefully to their rest. The ones that remained, I hoped I could give them peace.

I tried to remember how I'd done it up at the lake, but after sitting there for more than five minutes, my inherent impatience got the better of me.

"How am I supposed to do this?" I asked, my eyes still closed as I tried to figure my shit out.

I could hear the exasperation in Hildy's voice when he answered, "You're supposed to call them to ya, lass. With your mind. Invite them to move on. It shouldn't be too hard."

He said that, but I didn't see him sending souls to their final rest.

Huffing, I tried to open my mind, to see the souls coming to me. A cold touch fluttered over my hand, and I opened my eyes. A brunette ghost, about my age when she'd passed, had approached. She gave me a beaming smile, and then she moved to hug me.

Instead of a hug, she seemed to fall into me, the faint kiss of her memories touching my mind as my aches eased. Her name was Margaret and she'd died of... sepsis from a cut on her hand. The details of her life were faint, as if the time she'd spent as a ghost leached them away from her.

The next soul to approach seemed less benign, he scratched at his face, flickering in and out of sight. He seemed in pain, like he was trying to come to me, but his body wouldn't let him. Mentally, I pulled at him, reeling him in. All it took was one touch, and he fell into me. His name was Tobias, and he'd been a businessman of some kind. A store owner maybe. He'd lost his life to a robbery, shot dead in the middle of a store as his killer stole his money.

As soon as he fell into me, all he felt was relief. He'd left a wife and daughter behind, but they were long dead. He couldn't figure out how to follow them.

I absorbed three more souls before I felt a hand on my shoulder.

"It's time to stop," Bishop whispered in my ear, his voice sounding so far away.

I wanted to answer him, but there were more people who wanted out of this realm. They wanted out of their misery. Being stuck here with no family was hurting them. They missed their people. They wanted to rest.

I tried to articulate this to Bishop, but I couldn't. It wasn't time to stop.

Taking another soul, I felt the burn and realized too late that Bishop had been right. I was taking too much.

A group of specters were gathered in a small huddle in front of me. Some of them couldn't speak anymore, some were agitated and could turn. I felt horrible for them—caught between two worlds with no way out.

"I can't take you," I whispered, the regret hurting my heart, "but I'll be back. You'll get rest soon. I promise."

I had never made a promise like that to a ghost. I never promised them anything. There was something daunting about keeping a promise to someone who had already died. It meant really keeping it because there was nothing else for them to do but hound you until you did.

Promises to the dead were dangerous.

Most of the specters nodded and wandered off, but a few lingered, maybe hoping I'd change my mind. When I didn't, they stormed off in huffs of rage, luckily not having the power to turn even if they were of a mind to. No one had thought of these people in centuries—no one had lent them power. For that, I was really, really grateful.

Despite how good I felt elsewhere, the burn in my chest was a little concerning. It didn't hurt exactly, but there was an aching pull to it that had me up and off the stone bench. The only upside to the whole thing was that even though my chest felt like I'd eaten one too many carnitas, the rest of me felt great. Coupled with the fact that I wasn't glowing, and I was coming up aces.

But something was calling me forward, out from under the willow and out in the cemetery proper. Sarina and Bishop called my name, but their voices had a far-off quality, as if they were underwater. Slanted headstones and crack monuments littered the small space. The grass was overgrown in a lot of spots, and the moss was out of control.

This was a quiet place, a place where even the wind was still, and the birds didn't sing. I knew I was alone, but that didn't concern me. The burn in my chest, though, that did. The silence filled me with a bit of peace. Well, I thought that, and then the call of a raven scared the absolute shit out of me, making me jump.

Perched on a cracked headstone, it's blue-black feathers almost shimmered in the sunlight. It cocked its head at me before it resettled itself. I'd never seen a raven up close and had no idea how fucking big they were. The bird cawed at me again, its wings shivering a second before it took flight, soaring up and circling around before diving for the ground.

A second before it looked like the raven would hit the ground, the air seemed to shimmer around it, and then the raven wasn't a bird anymore.

It was a man.

I managed a single gulp before I got myself under control.

"Hello, Azrael."

Azrael appeared less unkempt than the last time I'd seen him. Long gone were the ratty clothes and scraggly locks. His hair had been cut at some point, the ends landing about shoulder-length, and with it out of his face, I could glimpse a long scar that cut around his left eyebrow and followed the curve of his cheek, stopping at his jaw. He'd selected a dark suit to wear, the color imposing more than I'd thought it would be.

But he was the Angel of Death. I couldn't see him wearing rainbows and glitter.

I had no idea if he could change his appearance at will or if he'd had to procure those duds, but the result was a slight bit more intimidating than I had planned for. In my head, I'd assumed he was likely still in his prison, and it would be a mind-meld sort of situation. Him being in the flesh was a bit more daunting.

"Hello, Darby," he murmured, his voice a crooning sort of calm that seemed honed out of eons of practice calming the newly deceased. "I hear you wanted to speak to me."

I gulped for real then. "From who?"

The absolute last thing I needed was to get ambushed in the middle of Haunted Peak.

Azrael gave me a gentle smile, shaking his head. "No one. I possess the ability to sense my children—especially when they wish to speak to me. No one except your friends know where you are. You're safe here."

I wanted to feel warm and fuzzy, but people were dying. Plus, I just wasn't a warm and fuzzy kind of girl. Answers, though, those I could do.

But although I had the prospect of answers right in front of me, my mind went blank. I didn't know where to start. Did I lead with what Mariana had done, or the un-nested vamps killing people, or his children killing each other for sport? I could ask how he'd been for the better part of last year, but everything just seemed too...

"Trivial?" he supplied, plucking the thought from my mind as his smile grew wide. "Your concerns aren't trivial. I think they are rather important. It has been a long time since I've spoken to one of my children—especially one so concerned about..." He paused, seeming to search for the word, "the welfare of the dead."

"They don't stop being people when they die. They're still them. They still have wants and needs and business to attend to. Death doesn't change that. It just makes the important stuff sift to the top of the bullshit."

Azrael gave me another smile like I'd just said something cute, which earned him a frown from me. I wasn't cute. I was odd, and I liked that about myself. He began to chuckle, which irritated me for no good reason. I guessed to him time didn't mean much. Death didn't mean much.

"It does," he insisted, his smile gone. "Death means quite a lot, actually. Maybe not the same way it does to you, but I am older than time and twice as tired. And perceptions change."

Hauling up my big girl pants, I asked, "Do you know who is trying to kill me? Or why?"

There was no finesse or pleasantries. I was a one-woman wrecking ball, and he was the target.

Azrael's chuckle was bitter this time. "You know why, Darby. It's the same reason almost all of my children have died over the years. Power. Young ones want it, not realizing what a yoke it is. If they understood how heavy the burden of power was, they wouldn't want it. But you know, and you don't want anything to do with it."

I snorted. "Of course I don't. I have enough power as it is. I don't need more. I don't need anything—I don't *want* anything."

Azrael leaned against a crumbling monument, his chuckle reaching me, even though I had a feeling it was meant to be quiet. "And that is precisely why you have it. Others would burn themselves up, turn themselves into monsters. You, my dear, do neither. You give it away to people in need. You wonder if the souls in this cemetery will get peace. You honor the dead."

"Yeah, yeah. I'm a fucking saint. So, you know the 'whys,' but not the 'who,' then?"

Were my words brash? Maybe. But I disliked when people avoided my questions—even if they were timeless death deities who could crush me like a bug.

He began laughing, the sheer joy of his mirth making tears roll down his face. Was it a little like a chihuahua barking at a grizzly bear? Kinda. At least this grizzly found me funny.

"You are refreshing, Darby Adler. I'm glad you are still among the living."

Time to wake up, kid. There's no resting yet. Not for a while.

Those words echoed in my brain, the familiarity of his voice sounding like a gong in my head.

"I take it you're the reason for that." Even healed, the realization hit me hard enough I needed to sit down. I planted my jeans-covered ass on the ground so I didn't pass out. "I died, didn't I?"

Azrael's laughter subsided. "In a way, yes. But just for a moment. It wasn't your time. I made it so you wouldn't leave before then."

I was glad I was sitting down for that one. "What does that mean?"

Was that my voice that sounded like a child? Yes, it sure was.

"It means you didn't die before your time. Simple as that."

My irritation got the better of me. I swear, I had no intention of yelling at a death deity, honest. "That's not what you said. I interrogate murderers for a fucking living, Pops. Don't try to skirt the issue with me. What did you do?"

His narrowed eyes and flinty smile did not spell good things for my survivability in this situation. Not. One. Bit.

"I fixed it. That's what I did. Most people would be grateful."

"Most people don't want the mercurial nature of Fate to carry on undisturbed. They want what they want when they want it and fuck everyone else. I am not most people."

He snorted, and gave me a look that said, "No shit."

No wonder he and Mariana got on so well—or at least well enough to make a kid. They both were a pair of no-answering, skirting-around-the-issue irritants who loved to piss me off.

"Hey, that's not fair," he said, reading the insult from my thoughts. "I'll answer your questions."

"Good," I grumbled and started shooting off questions rapid-fire. "Who had the un-nested attack the ABI? Why were you entombed under a fucking mountain? Why does my mother think there is a throne for me to take? What did you do to me in that ravine that has you so cagey? Which one of my siblings wants me dead?"

Azrael huffed. "I don't have the answers to most of that." He held up a hand when I opened my mouth to protest. "But I'll answer what I can."

I quickly closed my trap and waited for him to continue.

"I don't know why the un-nested vampires were called to the ABI building. I can only assume since none of those souls have made it to me. Like you, I believe they were summoned for a targeted attack on both you and Mariana. Possibly to cut off your resources if they were unable to capture you or your information."

I wanted to growl, but I held my tongue. My hissy fit wouldn't do anyone any good.

"As for my imprisonment, well..." He trailed off, wincing. "I believe the reason I was interred was not the official statement. I believe I was locked away so your sibling could maneuver without my interference." He frowned then, an emotion ravaging his face for a moment before it was gone. "I do regret my actions, though. I did not kill my children, of course, but while it was in my power to prevent them from killing each other, I did not. It was the only reason I went willingly."

Then it all became clear. Azrael couldn't be killed. He couldn't be imprisoned. He couldn't be held. Not without his consent.

He was never in a cage.

"Correct," he confirmed, his gaze on my face. "I'll ask you a question so you may understand. Can you hold death in your palm? Can you see it? Can you stop it? Why would anyone believe they could lock it away?"

Because they were fools. Fools with a delusion of grandeur unbefitting the known reality.

"See? You get it. Your friend Jimmy has it right, though. I went back to my cell willingly when you asked because you needed to call your father forth. You needed to believe in something—in what you were doing so you had the strength to bring him back. I know you are my child, but Killian Adler raised you. I am not so proud that I would deny his role in your life. Just like you, it was not his time. It was hers, though."

Tabitha.

I still didn't regret taking her life. I wondered if that made me evil, if I was on the road to becoming something vile.

"Not at all. Tabitha—as you knew her—deserved to leave this world. You saved countless souls by denying her poison from the earth. What she wanted, what she was trying to accomplish by raising me? It would have meant an end to the order of things."

"She wanted the throne. Your throne."

Azrael nodded, but gave me a sly grin. "Funnily enough, she would never have been able to take it. Power of that magnitude? It would have burned her up from the inside out. Either way, she was dead—it was only a matter of time."

"But—"

"I said what she wanted would mean the end, not

what she would have been able to accomplish. She might have survived that time and tried again. She might have tried again and again, consuming souls left and right until she cut a swath through an entire population. Who knows what she would have tried to steal to attain that power? A spurned woman is a very dangerous being."

I shuddered. It was bad enough to think about Tabitha diddling my dad, but I wanted to gag when I pictured her and Azrael together. Was there such a thing as mind bleach?

"Not me." Azrael shuddered. "I believe one of your brothers."

Still disgusting, but at least I wouldn't be picturing it.

"I believe that is where she got the idea in the first place. She was an acolyte of one of my children. Believed that she would one day be at the right hand of Death himself. Not realizing that the children who desire my throne care for nothing and no one but power. She started out as a misguided young woman. She died a monster."

"And that's what my siblings are? Monsters?"

Azrael smiled, his grin stretching wide to reveal blindingly white teeth and a double set of upper and lower fangs. I doubted he was showing me them to scare me, but they did all the same. Quickly he sobered, his gaze getting the same far-off quality Sarina's did when she was searching the future. "Not all of them. You have a sister out in the world somewhere. She's not a monster, even though she thinks so. I have a feeling you'll be finding her soon enough. Many of the ones who were torn from this earth were innocent. They had no idea of their lineage, nor possessed the power to be a threat. It didn't stop your siblings from murdering them, anyway."

It hurt my heart to think of all the lives that had been stolen for a stupid bid for power. What did more power get anyone, anyway? More heartache, that's what.

"How many siblings are we talking about here? One? A million? Somewhere in between?"

"Alive? I'm not sure. I believe it's just the two, but there could be more."

At that, I raised an eyebrow. I mean, could the man have used a condom. Like once?

Azrael chuckled. "Yeah, I know. Keep it zipped next time. Got it. To my credit, it was a lot of women over an exceedingly long period of time."

I held up a hand. "I really don't need to know the details."

Azrael's gaze got that far-off quality again, like he was listening to something I couldn't hear.

"It's time for you to go. There is a problem for you to fix."

I stood. "What about you?"

He smiled at me. "Don't worry about me. I'll be around."

It was tough to reconcile the image of Azrael turning into a raven and flying away in my brain. I knew I saw it, sure. Intellectually, I was aware of shifters turning into animals, and sure, I'd seen them transform a time or two. But when Azrael did it, it was as if you could shake your head and just assume it was all a dream.

Maybe it had been.

If it hadn't been for the black feather resting against the toe of my Chuck's, maybe I could have believed it was all one long fever dream.

A hand closed around my upper arm, startling me. It really shouldn't have. The buzz of souls around me was as loud as ever.

"Darby?" Bishop called softly in my ear, and I

managed to peel my gaze from the feather. Bishop looked different. His skin, his hair, his whole self, had an extra something about them. Like a light but not. I couldn't put my finger on it. "You've been out here a while. Are you okay?"

I frowned. My talk with my father hadn't seemed that long, but I had a feeling reality and Azrael didn't exactly go hand in hand. "I'm fine. All fixed up. Just for curiosities sake, you did see me talking to a man out here, right?"

Bishop shook his head, concern etched on his face. "I saw you walk out here and sit down on the ground. You looked like you were talking to someone, but all I saw was a raven."

Once again, Azrael was a sneaky, sneaky death deity. The last time we'd spoken, no one could hear our conversation, and they all looked at me like I was a nutter. Nodding, I bent and retrieved the feather. Just like the raven had, the feather shimmered a bit at the edges, an iridescence to it that spoke of twisted realities and magic.

"You see the shimmer on this, right?" I asked, still examining the feather.

Bishop stared at the feather in my hand for a moment before sliding his gaze back to me. "I don't see anything but a feather. However, I can feel the magic rolling off of it. You were talking to a man, you said?"

"Azrael. We can skip the trip up the mountain. I got about all I'm going to get out of him for now. He said there was a problem for me to fix?"

Bishop shook his head in confusion. "Other than your siblings trying to kill you? No, I don't know of another problem on our docket."

Over Bishop's shoulder, I spied J striding out from under the willow tree, his pace almost a jog.

"It's time to go," he called, stopping as he waved at us like he was on a flight line ushering in a 747. Even from here, the only way I could describe his face was frantic.

Houston, I have found our problem.

Following J, Bishop and I raced through crumbling headstones and patchy grass back to the willow where Sarina was pacing like she'd just gotten a heavy bit of bad news.

Face screwed up in a frown, she was massaging her temples as her head twitched erratically.

Bishop went right to her, making her sit down on the bench. "Tell me what you see, Sarina."

His voice was calm and soothing, like this wasn't a new song and dance. Like he'd done this many, many times before.

She hissed, curling in on herself like her brain hurt. "Attack," she whispered, the word sounding like it took far too much effort to say. "Bigger than the ABI building one. Attacking the Dubois nest." She gasped for breath, the exertion almost too much for her. "Killing Magdalena and her second. Showing themselves to humans. Murdering them. Blood in the streets, running in rivers." Sarina sucked in a huge breath before she whispered the thing everyone with a functioning brain stem wanted to avoid. "War."

Bishop rubbed her back. "That's good information. How much time do we have? Days, weeks?"

"Hours. Maybe less than that." Sarina shook her head. "No time. No time."

Fuck.

Everyone else was strapped to the gills, but me? I was in a T-shirt and jeans, and not at all prepared to storm the fucking castle.

I dove for my duffle. By her tone, I knew we were going to fall in the "less" column. I yanked off my Ramones T-shirt and strapped my vest on over my tank top. The T-shirt went right back on and my holster went over it. After seating both of my weapons, I dug through the bag and found three blessed rosaries. I dropped each one around my neck and stuffed them down my shirt. Then went the backup M&P inside the spine holster. My leather jacket went over the whole ensemble, and I prayed that the spells in the leather held up. After nine months of no use, I held little hope, but maybe protection spells like the ones infused in this jacket got stronger over time.

Yeah, even I knew I wasn't that lucky.

Sarina was rocking on the bench as she hugged herself. Her small fingers dug into the skin of her arms, and I wedged a finger in between her palm and arm, pulling her hand away.

"Sarina, darling," I called, kneeling at her feet. "Come on back now. You warned us. Now it's time to go to work, okay? Can you pull yourself out?"

Sarina might be the most prolific psychic I'd ever dealt with, but she wasn't the first. There were quite a few with the gift in the Knoxville coven, though their witch magic usually conflicted with their sight. Sarina had to be a full-blooded psychic to see as well as she did.

"Oracle, dammit. I'm an oracle." Sarina's gaze finally lost its thousand-yard stare and focused on me.

I chuckled. "There she is. What do you say? Wanna go save a master vampire before the government bombs us off the face of the map?"

I wasn't stupid. I knew once the government figured out that they weren't at the top of the food chain, the bombs would drop on us. Sure, it wouldn't work. Sure, it would cause an all-out bloodbath. But they'd try it. I did not need any more ghosts on my hands.

No, thank you.

"We don't have a lot of time," she whispered.

Awesome. My gaze caught on J, and my stomach dropped. No way did I want him walking into a vampire nest on the brink of war.

"It's time for you to go, J," I insisted, snagging his sleeve. The images of what could happen to him flashed through my brain. It was bad enough I would be walking in there. If he followed me... I shuddered to think what could have happened if I'd failed at the lake. If I could prevent that, I would. "You aren't coming with us."

J stared down at my hand on his sleeve before meeting my eyes. "Are you going?"

He was my best friend and one-hundred-percent human. He didn't have extra anything that gave him an edge. If he followed me into this shit, he was going to get himself killed.

"You know damn well I'm going. But I'm not human. You are. This isn't like when we were kids, and you could do all the same shit I did. This is blood and death and beings who could rip you in half, drink you down, and laugh while they do it."

"Are. You. Going?" he repeated.

"God fucking dammit, J," I shouted, because I knew.

He'd made up his mind, and there wasn't a damn thing I could do about it short of hog-tying him and locking him in my fucking trunk.

I searched the faces of everyone else, landing on Jimmy. "Care to help me out here?"

Jimmy just shrugged at me, which was fair. He didn't have any more say than I did. I knew I should have set them up earlier.

"A man must make his own fate, lass," Hildy murmured, earning a growl from me.

"Fine," I growled, "but I swear if you get killed, I'm probably going right back to prison for bringing your stupid ass back to life. Or..." I trailed off, thinking about the death deity I had for a father. I shook my head. I couldn't scold him for whatever shit he pulled bringing me back and beg for someone else's life.

Of course, that didn't mean I wouldn't be changing my mind on that front if something went awry.

"Whenever you're done having a hissy fit," Bishop prompted, motioning for us all to gather close.

A shade-jumping adventure.

Super.

Daylight hit the alley different from the last time I'd seen it. It was still bright colors and superclean, but the air had a silence to it that was more than a little disconcerting. After making sure my stomach stayed inside my body, we followed the building around the corner to the cathedral steps, the deserted Knoxville street sending ice through my veins.

J and I yanked our sidearms free in tandem. Blame it on damn near a lifetime together, but we knew a hostile situation when we saw one. A deserted street, silent birds, not so much as an errant pedestrian... yeah. Bad shit was going to or had already gone down.

Sarina knocked on the cathedral door, the booming echo of her small fist hitting the wood making me struggle to swallow. Never—not once—had someone failed to be on these steps, had someone failed to answer, had someone not already been at the door to let me in.

"Open it," I said, my voice pitched low.

I was staring at Hildy, wanting him to do his mojo, but he shook his head. "I can't, lass. Only Dubois blood can open that door."

Shit. Did I even have Ingrid's number?

"God fucking dammit all to hell," Bishop growled, shouldering through us. He hesitated before placing his hand on the intricately carved doorknob. Sighing heavily, he turned the knob as easy as you please.

Umm... excuse me? What in the unholy fuckery is this?

Sarina snorted before quickly sobering when Bishop shot her a look. "Not one word."

I wanted to open my mouth anyway to ask, but it was not the time. I mean, it did sort of explain how Bishop could walk out of the Dubois nest without so much as a scratch after giving a major "fuck you" to Mags. Still...

Bishop's magic flowed over his hands as he opened the door. Taking point, he went in first, then it was J and Sarina, Jimmy and Hildy, and then me. The Dubois nest was silent as the grave, but even though I couldn't see anyone, I knew it wasn't empty. The buzz of their souls was louder than a kicked beehive. I could practically feel their souls calling to me.

They were gearing up for something big, and if they were in the hiding portion of the festivities, it couldn't be good.

"Mags, Ingrid, someone come talk to me," I shouted, my voice echoing off the open space. "You have trouble coming and hiding isn't going to do the trick."

It seemed they were already aware, but what the hell else was I supposed to say?

A tiny blonde vampire raced for me, stopping only after she'd shouldered through my compatriots. "About time you got here. We got word un-nesteds were headed this way. You got better intel, I'm all ears."

It was very tough to forget that Ingrid was essentially a general and had commanded more armies than I knew what to do with.

Sarina stepped up. "Their goal is to take out your queen and her second. The number is almost double that of the ABI attack, so around a hundred or so. We don't have much time. They will find a way to breach."

"Yeah, that's better than my intel. We still got the word out to some of our thralls in the KPD. They cleared the area." Ingrid rubbed at her face as if she'd been worked to the bone. "We fortified the wards, called in favors. Shiloh is on her way, but I don't know if it will be enough."

I tried to think about the level of damage a hundred un-nested vampires could do. Blood in the streets wasn't even the half of it. But breaching this place...

"Hildy made it seem like anyone at that door would sit out there until Judgment Day if they weren't of Dubois blood." Did I look at Bishop when I said this? No, I did not. "Is there another entry point, or do you have an internal problem?"

Ingrid huffed. "Door number two."

22

An internal problem in the Dubois nest wasn't exactly a new thing. More than once Mags had been forced to remove members who refused to follow the rules. Some—unhappy with their position—had decided to leave on their own. Magdalena wasn't prone to beheadings or fits of pique and was of the opinion that executions made more enemies than it eliminated.

She sure as hell shot herself in the foot with that bit of mercy. Not that I wouldn't have done the same.

"Jimmy, you got any warding mojo in your bag of tricks?" What the elf could and could not do was a solid unknown to me. The fact that he lived in town, had a human job, and loved electronics more than some people loved their children, made him the least elf-like Fae I'd ever seen. Not that I'd seen many.

The tall man shuffled his feet and met my gaze. "Not warding, exactly. I can make the majority of them lose the building, though. Like they'd look at it and their eyes would just slide off. It won't keep them out, but it'll slow them down."

I shot my eyes to Ingrid. "That work for you?"

She chuckled like I'd just said something funny. "Any help at all is welcome. If it keeps my queen alive, I'm all for it. The last thing I need is to take the mantle. I swear that woman deals with more headaches in a day than I do all year." Her gaze flicked from me to Bishop. "She's glad you came. I know you don't like us, but she cares about you."

That was a hell of a one-eighty from the last time they'd spoken, and I had to wonder what the fuck was going on with Bishop and the Dubois nest.

But Bishop didn't meet my eyes. Instead, he followed Jimmy and the pair of them reinforced the wards. Not that his non-answer was of any consequence. As old as Magdalena was, she could have been the first vamp turned in her line. Meaning, even as young as she was when she was turned, she could still have living relatives. That would actually make a hell of a lot of sense.

"Is there an exit strategy?" J asked, his eyes still wide as saucers as he stared at the tiny enforcer. "A fallback plan if the breach is too advanced?"

I was waiting for Ingrid to start cussing like a sailor just so I could watch J get all scandalized. I swear that would make my whole year. Plus, I doubted he'd ever met a vampire before, add in the fact that Ingrid was less than half his size made it all the better. I hadn't exactly elaborated on the details of the arcane world.

Ingrid nodded as she held in her grin by the skin of her teeth. The last thing J needed to see was a set of fangs. "The crypts and cemetery. It leads to a secluded spot with very little human presence. But if the fight spills much past there, we're going to have a problem. KPD has only cleared three blocks. It would take pulling strings we don't have for more."

Sarina yanked a slim phone from her back pocket. "Let me see if I can yank those strings, shall I?"

"Weapons? Warriors?" I was trying to think of anything I could do to help them, and other than absorbing a shit-ton of souls and blowing everything up, I was at a loss for what I could offer. My gaze fell on Hildy. "You got any tips?"

Hildy twirled his cane in his hand before bowing at the tiny general. "Hildenbrand O'Shea, lass. May I offer some advice on your crow's nest and sentry points?"

Ingrid stood stock-still for about five seconds before her eyes flashed red. "You're Hildy?" she breathed. "*Hildy* is Hildenbrand O'Shea?" she accused, spearing me with a glare so fierce, if she weren't my friend, I'd be positive she was about to murder me.

"Did I forget to mention that?"

Ingrid growled under her breath as she let Hildy lead her away to discuss where to put her snipers, which left J and I in the middle of an almost-deserted cathedral waiting for an attack. I didn't know exactly how I was supposed to help. I sort of figured that if push came to shove, I could reap whatever souls were left in the graveyard and vaporize people, but I worried that it would be sort of like trying to fill a shot glass with a tsunami.

Plus, I'd never done the whole reaping thing around the undead. All in all, it sounded dicey as fuck.

I pulled J by the sleeve, deeper into the decommissioned church, wanting him to meet Mags before everything went to shit. But I didn't find her. I did, however, find a ton of mid-level vamps ushering the younger ones out of the nest through a series of tunnels that ran through the basement. It made sense to me, but J, I could tell, had questions.

"Our ex-fil is above ground to prevent the tunnels from being discovered. I'll bet anything that they'll blow the entrance to the tunnels as soon as the attack comes."

J smiled. "Sneaky. I like it."

"So glad you approve," a low voice said, and I turned to find Magdalena outfitted to the gills in weapons and armor. Unlike her general, she was in head-to-toe tactical gear. Black combat boots, black tac pants, likely bulletproof vest, and a platinum cuff around her neck. The cuff reached from just under her jawline past her collarbone and down her chest, and she had a pair of matching ones on her wrists. Across her back was a quiver full of arrows—likely spell-tipped—and a bow. At her left hip was a pair of katanas, stacked one on top of the other, and at her right was what looked like a Glock.

"Your general going to get outfitted like you anytime soon?" I asked, admiring her hardware.

Mags shrugged. "She says that she has gone into battle naked with nothing but her fangs and talons, and she likes it that way. Says no one can steal a weapon off you if you don't have one to steal. I swear, that child will be the death of me."

Only Magdalena would call a two-thousand-year-old vampire a child.

"Mags, please meet Jeremiah Cooper, my partner."

"Ah, the infamous J." Mags gave him a wide smile that showed him every single one of her needlelike fangs. "Dipping more than a toe in this world, aren't you? I take it you declined to sit this one out?" She tutted at him like he was a naughty boy. "Careful, pet. You need all your body parts if you're to be turned, you know."

With that little bit of censure, she glided off to handle whatever it was she needed to handle.

J had gone white as a sheet, and I had to swallow a laugh—totally inappropriate given the situation, I know —but it was funny.

J pivoted on his heel and stared at me with the widest of eyes. "Turned?"

I couldn't help it, I snickered. "Into a vampire or a ghoul. She's telling you to make sure you keep all your body parts attached in the event of your death."

"How in the fuck am I supposed to do that?"

"Beats me. The one time I did it, I couldn't say I was too concerned about any of my parts being intact."

J growled at me with enough ferocity that a couple of the older vamps paused to stare. I waved them off, doubting J would choose to kill me now. If he hadn't before, I doubted that one quip was going to do it.

"When this is over, you and I are going to have a full conversation about what the fuck has been going on for the last nine months." When I opened my mouth to volley back, he shushed me. "No. I'm not taking any shit off you this time. We're having it. And I'll be sure to go over what the fuck you were thinking in that goddamn ravine while I'm at it, too. Until then, as your best friend, I formally request that you refrain from doing stupid shit until the rest of forever. How'd that be?"

He was asking this now? On the precipice of fucking battle with an un-nested army? By very definition this whole gig was one huge dumb move that was likely going to get my ass killed.

"How about you ask me to stop doing stupid shit tomorrow? Deal?"

J grumbled, rolling his eyes at me. Then he dragged me into a hug so tight, I was lucky my ribs were healed, or he would have smashed them to smithereens.

"Don't get dead," he whispered in my ear.

"You either. Because I will totally make Mags bring you back as a vamp, and if that doesn't work, I'll make Bishop bring you back as a ghoul." I didn't add that if that didn't work, I was in good with a death deity, so he was staying if I had anything to say about it.

Pushing off of him, I checked my weapons, making sure I was covered.

"You have enough ammo?" I asked, wondering where Bishop ran off to with my duffle. There was never, ever going to be enough ammo when it came to dealing with vamps.

Said death mage was jogging our way, but he didn't have Jimmy with him. He slid my duffle across the floor, and it stopped at the toes of my Chucks. I dove for the remainder of my weapons as he began giving J a briefing. "Vamps are tricky targets. They move faster than you can see, so you want to hit one when they are still or busy. You need to take the head or the heart. Body shots do fuck all. Personally, I'd prefer you to be in a sniper position, but truth be told, those are the easiest to pick off because they're secluded, and vamps can hear where the shots come from."

He paused, and I looked up to find Bishop staring down at me.

"Please tell me you have spelled rounds. I don't have the time to make any."

I wanted to be plucky and cool, but I just didn't have it in me. "Not enough. Not with a hundred or so vamps coming in here."

Truth be told, there would never be enough.

The reality of the situation hit me like a ton of bricks. We shouldn't be here. We should be following the young ones through the tunnels and getting the hell out of here.

We should be running.

Then the memory of Sarina's voice as she wailed out her premonition tore through my brain.

Blood in the streets. Rivers of it.

"There's no one we can call, is there?"

One look at Bishop's face was all I needed to get my answer.

Because the answer was no.

23

I thought there would have been more warning. Even with the wards Jimmy and Bishop put in place, I sort of thought the buzz of a hundred vamp souls would have been louder. Would have called to me like a siren song of impending death. But they were more silent than any grave I'd ever come across.

The first breach came from a single arrow crashing through the pane of one of the stained-glass windows. The spelled arrowhead embedded into the wood of a pew only a few feet from our huddle. The arrow had to be spelled, right? There was no other way it could have sailed through Bishop and Jimmy's wards, not to mention whatever security the Dubois nest already had in place.

At the first break in the glass, both J and I drew our

weapons, the welcome weight of a gun in my hand seeming to slow everything down for me.

"Get back behind the dais," Magdalena ordered, moving in front of us as she drew an arrow from her own quiver. "Take cover and be prepared to move."

She then nodded at the vamp who was acting as sentry in front of the tunnel entrance. He gave her a hesitant nod, the reluctance on his face plain as day before pressing a red button on the device in his hand. Getting the majority of their young ones out made Mags so much different from other monarchs—or at least from what I'd heard. In European nests, their young ones were cannon fodder, a way for the old to keep right on trucking through the years without so much as a scratch. Mags didn't play that way, and it made me like her so much more than I had before.

I couldn't feel the concussion at first, but the blast soon ricocheted through the whole of the decommissioned church, nearly bending the solid-steel blast doors.

Unlike the rest of us who ducked for cover, Mags was unmoved by the blast. Drawing back her arrow, she aimed for the tiny break in the glass. Letting it fly, it sailed through the small hole like she'd done it a thousand times before. I had to say, the answering scream following the arrow hitting its mark was supremely satisfying.

For that one shining moment, I had hope—a whole boatload of it. Hope that this battle wouldn't mean the end of a nest I'd put myself in hot water to help. That we would win, and this trouble would soon be behind us. That my friends would all walk away with breath still in their lungs.

Until ten spelled arrows answered Magdalena's, cutting through one of the side windows, like a knife through butter.

Until one of the arrows found a home in Mag's stomach.

Until Mag's scream echoed through the cathedral like an omen of death.

Blood spilled from her wound, but she didn't go down. Shakily, she grabbed the rune-carved wood, yanking it out. As soon as the arrowhead left her body, Mags went rigid, her back straightening as if someone had pulled the string of her spine.

Ingrid dove for her queen—without armor, without weapons, without anything—ready and willing to drag her to safety. The arrow clattered to the floor right as Ingrid reached Mags, but Ingrid never got the chance to pull Magdalena to safety.

"Get back," Mags growled, and quick as a whip, her

arm shot out, slamming into Ingrid's small face with the force of a wrecking ball. "Ssstay away from me."

Magdalena clutched at her own head as Ingrid sailed the few feet toward us, landing hard on the marble floor. Ingrid's face was a bloody, broken mess as she lay crumpled at our feet. But the tiny general didn't stay down long. Oh, no, she was up and ready to try to reach her queen again until Jimmy managed to snag her by the middle. Just about the only thing that saved Jimmy's life were the words that dumped ice water in all our veins.

"There was a... spell on the arrow," he shouted, struggling with the Dubois enforcer. "Her mind... is not her own."

Mag's talons raked at the skin of her face, the regret there the only clue that she was fighting something. That fact was proven not a second later when Mags slowly staggered for the warded doors, her movements sluggish when I knew she could be faster than light if she had a mind for it.

Ingrid fought against Jimmy's hold as members of the nest raced for Magdalena, trying to prevent her from getting to the doors. As old as she was, there was little hope of them succeeding. Even as she fought her own mind, she still batted them away like gnats.

Magic lit over Bishop's hands as he stared at Mags.

"Someone needs to take her down," he muttered. "If she opens that door, we're fucked."

Ingrid managed to yank herself out of Jimmy's giant hold and turned her still-healing face to glare up at Bishop, her wounds closing before my eyes. "I suggest you keep that stupid-ass comment to yourself for the rest of your fucking life, Death Boy. Mags might give a shit that your grandmother made her, but I don't. If you value breathing, I suggest you learn to keep your mouth shut."

Bishop gestured at the melee in the middle of the cathedral. "And I suggest you jump in there and do something. No one else in this whole fucking nest is as old as you are or has a hope of stopping her. Hop-to, little bunny, before your boss decides to open the flood gates."

Growling, Ingrid raced through the throng of her nestmates to stop her queen from reaching the door, launching herself onto and off of the edge of a pew, landing a solid haymaker to Magdalena's temple. Mags swiped at her, but the tiny enforcer was too quick, prepared at last to tangle with her queen. There was a reason Ingrid was the general and Mags was the queen. In the written histories, Ingrid Dubois had not been bested in battle *ever*, and I seriously doubted she'd break that streak if she could help it.

The sound of glass breaking rent the air over the cacophony of vampires duking it out. Dozens of arrows sailed through the windows. The majority of our little group ducked, trying to avoid losing ourselves in the middle of this shitstorm. But a few vamps weren't so lucky. One took an arrow right through the chest, her death scream something of nightmares as her body withered before my very eyes, the damage to her heart absolute.

Other than Tabitha, I hadn't seen the transition from life to death; I hadn't seen a soul leave a body. The process was startling, her soul remained standing as her body fell away from it, landing on the ground in a heap of ash. Her ghost stared down at the scattered remnants of her corpse, unmoving.

The other two vamps that'd been hit, each ripped out their arrows in tandem as if they had no other choice—the first to his own detriment. His neck wound disabled him quickly as it ripped through his jugular. His friend was another story altogether, his straightened spine and jerky movements matching Mags' exactly as he lumbered toward the door.

This time, Bishop didn't ask permission—not that there was anyone to give him any. Instead, he shot a crackling ball of purple magic straight at the vamp. We all watched in wonder as the magic hit its target, the purple spell swarming the vamp as it made him crumple to the floor in a heap. Unlike his nestmate, he did not wither and die. Eyes opened and staring, he remained immobile and unharmed.

"You could have done that to Mags," I accused, stunned at his power over the vamp. At how much it reminded me of another time when I'd seen this kind of magic.

Bishop gave me a dark chuckle, shaking his head but not meeting my gaze. "Magdalena Dubois is almost three thousand years old. That spell wasn't going to cut it, and I like my head right where it is, thank you."

But I didn't have a frame of reference. I didn't know how old Bishop was, and the little tidbit about his grandmother making Magdalena did not escape my notice. I had a feeling Bishop wasn't just old. He was *old*.

The swarm of Dubois vamps clustered around the door, and I lost sight of Mags and Ingrid. I quickly found them again as ten nest members went flying, the answering screech of their queen drawing my gaze to the door.

They weren't going to be able to stop her from opening it. They weren't going to be able to keep the un-nesteds out.

More arrows sailed through the windows, hitting even more of the Dubois vamps. Bishop volleyed his mojo at the ones he could, but there were just too many. It didn't matter if there were snipers in the crow's nests picking them off, and it didn't matter that this place was warded out the ass. They were coming in whether we liked it or not.

"Fall back," Hildy ordered. Since his main mission in life—or death—was keeping me alive, I listened.

Following my grandfather through the cathedral halls, he led us to a courtyard. Or rather a graveyard. The small cemetery was surrounded by a fence that was stone on the bottom and wrought iron on top, the four-foot posts topped with sharp-looking arrows. Trees dotted the space, and the graves were carefully maintained, each with a blanket of wildflowers over them. The buzz of souls slid over me like a caress, the sight of shimmering specters lending me just a little hope in the middle of this shit.

It wasn't until my eyes landed on a group of vamps clawing at the iron bars did that hope die a very quick death. It irked me that I couldn't feel them. The Dubois nest was filled with an incessant buzzing, their souls practically yelling that they would be living long lives with no end in sight.

Then it dawned on me. What buzzed at me were souls. That sound buffeted me at all times, constantly scratching at my brain. But these arcaners didn't have a soul to buzz at me. It was why I'd been caught off guard when the arrows flew into the church, why I couldn't feel them at all.

Fuck.

With each rake of these vamps' talons, a spark of magic bloomed over the ward like a ripple in water.

"That ward isn't going to hold," Sarina said aloud just as I was thinking it.

A man elbowed his way to the front of the vamps. The suited man was familiar, a face I'd seen in the last day or so, but I couldn't place it. Bishop and Sarina gasped in tandem, their recognition plain as day.

Sandy-blond hair, chiseled jaw, a general frat-boy air about him. Yes, I had met him before. In the records room right before... Right before the ABI had been attacked. Right before Kevin had been killed. Right before those agents had been rounded up and murdered.

His name escaped me, but I remembered his face.

"Smith Easton," Bishop growled through clenched teeth, magic blooming in earnest over his hands as he lost his hold on his rage. The ground shook a little, as his anger rolled through the graveyard, the sky darkening to pitch in an instant.

Easton shot us an unrepentant grin as he flashed an intricate blade in his fist. Not much longer than my forearm, he made a show of twirling the knife before stabbing it in the shimmering ward, the sharp edge piercing the magic.

He ripped the blade through the spell as if it were nothing, smiling all the while, like a kid on Christmas morning.

The vamps' talons scrabbled at the edges of the ward like it was a tangible fence, clawing the sides back so they could get in. The sound of screams pierced the air behind us, the thunder of the sky above and feet below ricocheting through us all.

We were surrounded.

Easton swept through the broken ward and sailed over the fence, his crisp suit with nary a speck of dirt on it as he continued to twirl the blade in his hand. The twirl was meant as a taunt, an insult. Like he had all the time in the world, and he was drawing it out for kicks. All the while, I could hear him chuckling, the sound worse than any number of souls buzzing in my brain could ever be.

His gaze unerringly went right for me. Not to the murderous death mage, not to the giant elf, or the famed grave talker. Not to anyone else but me.

"He said you were so smart. He said you'd figure it out in no time. Said *you'd* come to *me*. He really did overestimate your abilities, didn't he?"

I t didn't take a rocket scientist to figure out that Smith Easton was not a man in charge. He was either following orders or trying to break out on his own—just like Tabitha had done.

Easton reached for the knot of his tie, loosening the fabric as he continued twirling that fucking knife, the purple of his magic snaking down the blade. It brought back memories of last year—of Tabitha's curved blade slicing through my father's chest. I'd dreamt of that knife more times than I could count. Dreamt of the rapidly cooling blood on my fingers as my father died in my arms.

That blade pissed me the fuck off.

Growling, I raised my weapon, the world seeming to slow with the weight of the gun in my hand. For that solitary moment, the ground ceased to tremble beneath my feet, the wind refused to blow. Time itself slowed to a crawl as I fired off a round, the bullet screaming through the air toward my target. But it didn't matter how good my aim was or the spell on the round, my bullet failed to hit its mark.

Easton's spinning blade batted away the round like it was nothing, like he could have done it in his sleep. Seething, I let loose, firing off one round after the other, each one kissing the metal of his knife. He rose a hand in the air, purple magic coating his fingers as he brought it down again. As several of the vamps let out barks of attack, their voices echoed through my bones, letting me know we were really, really screwed.

Easton had control over them all, the purple of his magics giving me a big fucking clue. Blood mage. Easton was a blood mage, and he not only was controlling these vamps, he'd also undoubtedly made them all, too.

"Fuck this shit," Bishop growled, the ground pitching in earnest as his power raced up his arms. The swirling black and purple magic seemed to have a mind of its own as it snaked all the way up to his neck before flowing from his fingers. Blood and death. That was what Bishop was made of, and he showed it.

Tree roots snapped as the ground broke apart. The edges of coffins rose to the surface as boney fists pounded at the lids. Reanimated corpses punched through the wood, crawling out of their resting places like skittering spiders.

I was not a fan of the zombie craze that had everyone else so enthralled. The absolute last thing I wanted to see when I was trying to relax in front of the TV was more dead bodies. I'd never been an avid horror movie buff either, so the sight of corpses coming to life and busting out of their graves kind of made me want to either run in the other direction, vomit, or both. And this came from a woman who looked at dead bodies for a fucking living.

It wasn't like I was a stranger to decomposition, but sweet Christ on toast, the smell of maybe fifty dead bodies busting from the earth at once was enough to put anyone off their lunch. Staggering to their feet, bones clacked and popped as they shuffled to their intended target. Vamps spilled through the break in the ward, up and over the fence, clashing with the risen dead.

With my gun useless against Easton, I holstered the weapon and closed my eyes. The very best I could do was call souls to me, after that it was a wag, but I'd work that out when I came to it. I felt the tether of the waiting souls like a physical thing. Each of the shimmering specters moved toward me, the world falling away from us as I beckoned them closer.

If you wish to move on from this world, come to me. I called these words in my mind, begging the souls to fill me with a power I hadn't felt since my time up at Whisper Lake. Begging these spirits that had tethered themselves to this plane far longer than their bodies had survived.

If not, please fight with us against those soulless monsters that would destroy me and mine. Fight. Please.

What had Hildy told me? All I had to do was picture it in my mind—all I had to do was think it. I wondered if that was the same advice he'd given my mother, or if that was singular to me. It didn't really matter anymore, now did it.

The first soul that filled me was of a priest that had died a couple of centuries past. His life was one of penance and sacrifice, and he'd died with a flock of parishioners who mourned his passing. The second soul refused to move on, backing away from me as if I were a demon. I couldn't taste her life on my tongue, but gleaned a glimpse of her soul, and given what I saw, she would be on this earth as long as she could cling to it.

Where she was going wasn't a good place.

The third, fourth, and fifth souls practically raced for me, hitting me with a one-, two-, three-punch of well-lived lives and a much-needed rest. They had lost their way to the other plane sometime in the last fifty years, failing to follow the call of my father's voice.

In the middle of all this—despite the power filling me, despite the burn in my limbs and chest—I wondered how many souls were out there that were too stubborn to leave, too stubborn to move on. More and more specters flocked to me, tens maybe close to a hundred in this small cemetery, fell into me to their rest, filling me with more power than I could possibly contain.

But it didn't matter how much power I had, I couldn't feel the buzzing of a soulless body. Easton and his vampires didn't have a soul for me to reap—didn't have a soul for me to call. I had no power over him or them. But I was willing to bet I had enough power over the dead to make a difference.

By the time I opened my eyes, the battle was in full swing. J and Sarina were taking headshots at vamps behind the cover of a solid stone bench. Bishop was tossing magic this way and that, commanding the reanimated bodies of the souls I'd just absorbed. Hildy was spinning up the remaining specters, angering them to the precipice of poltergeists to let loose on the soulless vampires.

But it was Jimmy who really caught my attention. I had no idea where he'd gotten the blade in his hands or where he'd learned how to fight with it, but Jimmy Hanson was no slouch with a broadsword. At six and a half feet of solid muscle, the giant Viking elf covered our six, mowing through vamps like he was born to do it. At his feet were the ashes of the vampires he'd already tangled with, the mounds of it collecting around him like snowdrifts.

Just like the last time I'd consumed too many souls for my body to hold, I was glowing and floating, light coursing over my flesh like a Lite Bright on steroids. A voice in my head begged me to act, begged me to use my power against the horde of vampires swarming us like bees. The voice sounded awfully like Sarina, but it was distorted, like an AM radio on the fritz.

Whether it was my friend or not didn't matter. It mattered that the plea was accurate. With or without a soul, did I not have power over the dead?

I was about to find out.

The burn of power coursed through my veins. The searing ache of too many souls, too much energy under my skin, raced like a molten flash fire just begging to be set free. My only option—unless I wanted to burn myself up—was to let this power loose. But unlike when I just gave it away to the witches near death, I molded it into a weapon.

It bloomed from my fingertips, the blindingly bright light falling from my hands like bolts of untethered energy. The first barb shot from my hands like a missile, hitting an advancing cluster of vampires like a flash fire.

The five vampires turned to ash on the spot, their bodies still in motion as they disintegrated.

The smile that flitted across my lips was not a nice one. I probably shouldn't feel good about people losing their lives, but I fucking well did. Letting my power loose, I whipped another barb of power at a cluster of reanimated corpses tangling with too many vamps to count. The zombies—for lack of a better word—were the only protection Bishop had while he was working his magic. The worry that I'd hurt his magic—or him— flitted around in the back of my mind as I cast my power out, but I shouldn't have worried. Seeming to have a mind of its own, the burning barbs of light caressed the zombies but full-on flambéed the vamps, turning them to ash in a single instant.

A wailing ghost ran full out toward a throng of vampires, the power in her rage enough to send them flying. As soon as they hit the ground, Bishop's freshly unbusy zombies attacked, stabbing through chests with their sharp bones or ripping off heads with their rotten hands.

But there were more vamps flowing through the break in the ward—far more than the hundred we'd been expecting—and I had no idea how we were supposed to hold them all off. Or what they were really after.

The second wave had come at last, and we were well and truly fucked.

Well, until it seemed like everything stilled at once. Some vampires in mid-swing, some mid-bite, some midair, the attacking vamps just stopped moving as if they were frozen in carbonite. Which made it really easy to find Smith Fucking Easton as he scrabbled toward the break in the ward.

He wasn't twirling that stupid blade now, now was he? But he didn't make it very far. The break in the ward was occupied by a tall brunette witch, with a smile of vengeance on her face.

Shiloh St. James. The buzz of her soul was loud in the frozen silence, along with the call of her coven surrounding us all.

"Late to the party, I see. What? You stop for fucking breakfast on your way here?" I asked her, more than a little grateful at her assistance, but holy fuck was she coming in at the tail end of this shit.

Shiloh spared me a glance long enough to stick her tongue out at me before her gaze relocked on Easton, the malice in it spelling out his end.

My feet hit the ground in a run. She couldn't kill him yet. I needed answers, and Easton was the only person who could give them to me. Shiloh raised her hand, the electricity of a spell blooming over her fingertips as a grin of pure death stretched her lips wide.

"Wait," I shouted, praying I reached her before she sealed his fate.

But Shiloh didn't stop. It was as if she either didn't hear me or refused to listen. Reaching across the scant space between them, she touched her electrified fingers to Easton's forehead.

He staggered back as he clutched his blade tighter in his hand. Without so much as a gurgle, he fought with himself as he raised the blade to his own neck. Without much thought on my part, I tackled the man, holding out a faint hope that I got to him in time. The pair of us rolled in the dirt, the blade knocked out of Easton's hand. He fought me, trying to reach for the knife—either to kill himself or me—but I was stronger.

Hands aglow, I latched onto his wrists, and the smell of smoldering flesh pervaded the air almost instantly. Easton howled in pain, but still fought me, his body squirming for the blade I could see out of the corner of my eye.

"Who sent you?" I growled, the question the only one I wanted answered. I could have asked him why, or what else they had planned, but that wouldn't tell me the threat.

Easton stopped struggling and looked me dead in the

face. Cocking his head in the dirt, he smiled. "X sends his best."

With a bolt of brilliant purple magic, he called the blade forth, the metal connecting with his hand in less than a blink. The glint of the knife was all I got to see before I was tackled from the side and thrown off Easton in a tangle of limbs.

At first, I couldn't tell who'd done the tackling. A fleeting glimpse of Bishop's face was all I got before the pair of us were up again, shoulder to shoulder, ready to fight.

But the fight was all but over.

By the time I got to my feet, Smith Easton was on his, meeting my gaze with a smile as he dragged the blade against his own throat. Before I could stop him, Easton began to crumble to ash, his face abrading away almost instantly as his body turned to dust. As soon as the last embers of Easton's body hit the ground, the vampires stuck in Shiloh's spell followed suit.

Mounds of ash blanketed the ground, and though I should have felt relief, I only felt a sense of dread. Yes, this battle was over, but the war was still waging. With Easton's soul gone, I had nothing to gain. No knowledge to glean.

It was tough to fight a war against an enemy you knew nothing about.

I wanted to rage, but everyone around me was cheering as if it was Victory Day. Bishop wrapped me up in a hug, and though I hugged him back, it all felt so hollow. None of this felt like a win to me.

It just felt like another defeat. Another unanswered question. Another dead lead.

Whoever my brother was, he sure as hell knew how to cover his tracks.

As soon as Bishop let me go, Shiloh pulled me into a hug. I couldn't help but be pissed at the Knoxville coven leader for her part in all this. If she wouldn't have worked that spell, if she would have just waited a second or two longer, I could have had the information I needed right now.

"We need to talk," Shiloh murmured in my ear, the gravity in her voice making me take notice.

"Soon," I replied, nodding as she released me from her embrace. We would be having a conversation one way or the other, and it damn well would be about what happened here today.

It took about half a second for me to start looking for J, and it took even less than that time to actually find him. Wrapped up in Jimmy's arms, my partner and my favorite elf were in a serious lip-lock that was so hot I felt scandalized from all the way over here.

"About damn time," I yelled, only to get flipped off by my partner as he just kept right on kissing the Viking dreamboat.

Dubois vampires began to emerge from the cathedral, most of them bloody messes, but the majority of them intact. Ingrid shouldered through the lot of them, her face a wreck of healing gashes, broken bones, and bald patches. Her left arm hung at her side in an awkward angle, while her right was busy holding an unconscious queen onto her shoulder. Ingrid dropped the queen at my feet before hauling back and slapping her right in the face.

The queen sucked in a huge breath, her eyes popping wide as her face bloomed red for a solitary moment before fading to her usual porcelain tone.

"What the hell was that for?" Mags griped, rubbing at her cheek.

"Oh, I don't know," Ingrid growled before snagging her left arm and yanking it back into place. "Maybe it's for not leaving the nest when I told you to. Maybe it's for not using the exit strategy I built ages ago to get to high ground. Maybe it's because you fucking bit off my pinky, you wench." Ingrid held up her child-size hand to show the regrowing digit. "Now you owe Darby and her whole fucking crew a boon—*each*—for saving your ass."

"What about me?" Shiloh asked. "Do I get a boon, too?"

Ingrid growled something under her breath. "No. I called you ages ago, and you just fucking got here. No boon for you."

"But—"

"I. Said. No." The tiny enforcer turned to Bishop. "Put those bodies back where they came from, or so help me, I will not be responsible for what I do next."

Bishop quickly took a step back. Given how disgruntled Ingrid was, he smartly didn't give her any lip. "On it."

Black and purple magic swirled in the air once again, the clacking bodies going to their rightful homes before their coffins repaired themselves and digging back under the ground. Hell, even the flower beds and headstones righted as if we'd never even been here.

Ingrid nodded at his good work, her sharp gaze inspecting the cemetery, likely looking for a reason to antagonize him. Coming up empty, she bid her thanks before taking her leave. "I need food and a bed. The young ones got the all-clear and should be back anytime now. They're in charge of getting all the rest of this shit fixed. You know where the exit is once you're ready to leave."

Ingrid and Magdalena bid us goodbye, the two of them hobbling together like a pair of old war buddies off to go get a drink.

"Lass?" Hildy called, and I peeled my gaze from my odd vampire friends to look at him. Appearing a little worse for wear, Hildy was sweating bullets as he kept hold of a group of particularly nasty poltergeists who were actively trying to bite his face off. "A little help here?"

"Please tell me those aren't what I think they are," Bishop whispered in my ear, seeing the phantoms for what they were. Regular ghosts weren't visible to just anyone. Poltergeist, though? Yeah, everyone got that frightening privilege.

"Oh, they are," Sarina quipped behind us, making the pair of us jump.

Bishop snagged the tiny oracle and yanked her into a hug. "Where the hell have you been? One second you're taking headshots, and the next you just disappeared."

"Vision," Sarina said as she shrugged, like that told us anything. "Had to hide for a little bit so I didn't get chomped on. Let's just say, we should clear out the stragglers and make sure this area is secure."

Bishop grumbled out his displeasure but followed her advice, ushering the milling vampires back inside the cathedral.

With his back turned, Sarina faced me.

"Call your father," Sarina urged, sending a wave of pure panic through me.

I yanked my phone from my back pocket, amazed I hadn't made it explode with my Lite Bright routine. She put a hand over my still-glowing fingers.

"Not Killian, the other one. Anymore souls in you, and we're going to have a problem. Hildy won't be able to help with these. They're too old and too vile. They don't want to leave."

The spirits held in Hildy's thrall were dark enough that I didn't have to consume them to know what they were made of. I couldn't imagine letting the slimy, oily things touch me, couldn't fathom how I could possibly stand it and not vomit.

"Good call." Closing my eyes, I sent out a mental

plea for help. Granted, *clean up on aisle one*, wasn't exactly asking nicely, but I'd rather not explode in a slew of Darby bits if I could help it.

The flutter of wings had me cracking a single eyelid, peeking through my lashes to see if my call had worked. Azrael's raven was perched on a nearby tombstone, his head cocked to the side to inspect me.

"Hiya, Pops," I quipped. "Any chance you want to reap those souls over there. I'd do it, but I'd rather not explode." I showed the bird my still-glowing hands. "Kinda having an issue here."

The raven cawed at me before taking flight again. In the same death-defying maneuver he'd performed before our last conversation, he dove for the ground, reforming into the shape of a man.

It didn't matter that I'd already seen it once, it still made me wince, hoping he didn't hurt himself. Yes, that made no sense. He was the personification of Death. What was he going to do? Keel over?

Azrael reformed at the last second into the besuited man that spoke to me in the cemetery in Haunted Peak. His chuckle was low and happy, as if he wanted to laugh outright but didn't want to irritate me.

"Exactly," he said, answering my thought as he was prone to do. "You have enough power in your hands to blow a hole in the world—not that you have the desire to be that stupid. You rang?"

My gaze snagged on my hands for a single second before flitting to the angry ghosts I had no desire to absorb. This whole situation reminded me of all the times I'd had my dad kill spiders in my room or check for snakes in my tent when we'd been camping—the nasty, vile tasks that befell fathers only on a cosmic level.

Azrael smiled, likely reading the analogy in my brain.

"Umm... help?" I asked stupidly, gesturing to the problem I had no idea how to fix.

"Ah... Hildy creating poltergeists again, is he?" Azrael observed, staring at the angry specters in Hildy's thrall. Hildy wouldn't be able to hold them too much longer. "You'd think he would have learned his lesson on that front, considering that's how he lost his life." Azrael shook his head. "I guess I'll let it go since it was for a good cause. Do remind him that he only has so many chances, though, will you?"

Mouth agape, I slowly turned from my father to Hildy. *Can't remember how he died, my ass.* No wonder he made shit up all the time, telling tall tales of his tragic demise. He got his ass killed by the very thing he was supposed to command. Wasn't that a kick in the junk?

Azrael let out another dark chuckle. "Don't tell him I told you. Hildy's mighty sensitive about that incident."

I mimed zipping my lips. No way was I going to drop that bomb on Hildy—not now, anyway. If that's how he'd gone out, it did make a fuck of a lot of sense why he'd gone so batshit in the aftermath of Greyson attacking me.

"Now you get it," Azrael murmured, nodding. "As prickly and stubborn and downright secretive as he is, Hildenbrand O'Shea would move heaven and earth for you. Try to keep him close, will you? It would help me sleep at night."

"You sleep at night?"

"Well..." Azrael trailed off, waggling his hand at me. "Not exactly, but the figure of speech is apropos."

Without another word, Azrael's hands began to glow as he locked his gaze on the specters. One by one, each specter was dragged by their feet to my father's waiting hands. As soon as a ghost was in reach, Azrael latched onto them, burning them up from their toes to their scalp.

It reminded me of the last time I'd seen a ghost die right before my eyes.

Tabitha.

The first ghost was nothing more than black motes in the air as he moved on to the next. The same as the first,

Azrael showed me exactly who death mages made their deals with. Death mages asked for Azrael's help in returning souls. Had to be. Azrael returned my father to me. Azrael helped me.

Tears gathered in my eyes, my heart full of gratitude at what he had done for me.

"You gave him back to me, didn't you?" I whispered. "Bishop did the spell, but you—you made it happen. You took Tabitha away. It was you."

Azrael dusted his hands off, a sly smile on his face. I brought a finger to his lips in the universal gesture for "shh."

"Let me know when you want lessons on how to deal with that," he said, gesturing at my hands, effectively changing the subject. "It's not like you can walk down the street glowing, Darby. Evidently, it's frowned upon."

Well, I had three guesses where my attitude came from and the first two didn't count.

"Cliff's Notes?"

Azrael's smile was small, but proud. "What does Hildy tell you? See it in your mind. Where do you want the power to go? In the air? In the earth? Does someone need help? Are there spells to be broken? Think about it. You have given it away before, yes?"

He was right. I had given it away. Closing my eyes, I searched for people in need. Most of the vamps were healed already, but there were a few that could use a boost. Bishop and J and Jimmy all had a few cuts and scrapes that could use some healing. Sarina had a migraine coming on that would knock her on her ass soon. It wouldn't kill her, but she needed some help. Without question, I gave her relief.

Bit by bit, I gave my power to others, chipping away at it until it could be contained. By the time I opened my eyes, Azrael was gone, a lone feather clinging to my Chucks the only proof he had been here at all.

Well, that and the missing poltergeists.

Bishop threaded an arm around my shoulders. "Meeting with your father again?" he asked, toeing the feather with his boot.

I reached down and snagged it. I couldn't say why I wanted to save it, exactly. Just that I needed to keep proof of him for some reason.

"Yeah," I whispered. "I guess I did."

"And that's what I've been doing for the last nine months," I finished with a flourish, ready for this part of J's interrogation to be over so I could go get ready. Unlike my kitchen, J's didn't have enough food or booze for a talk like this.

J insisted on this explanation before we went back to

work next week, and I'd been stalling like a champ. Who wanted to tell a woe-is-me story to their best friend? Definitely not this girl. But J needed answers, and though I didn't have all of them, I did explain the ones I had.

"Mariana Whatever-her-name-is-now needs to be launched from a canon into the desert where she can die a miserable, slow death."

"Now you're getting it. Can I be done now? Don't you have a date to go on?"

Reminding J of his upcoming date with Jimmy was just the right thing to make him quit talking about me. A smile I hadn't seen in some time spread over J's face, and he'd morphed into a giddy schoolboy, complete with dimples and a solid blush.

"Yeah." He sighed dreamily, and I was so happy for him, I thought I was going to burst from it. "I can't believe he just kissed me. I swear I could write a whole-ass romance novel out of that kiss." He put a hand to his chest like a swooning Southern woman. "And the sword fighting. Christ on toast, if I didn't think I was about to die, I would have let the vapors take me then. How did I not see how ridiculously gorgeous he is? Was I *blind*?"

I couldn't stop myself, I dissolved into giggles. J seemed just so scandalized that Jimmy was a certified beefcake, and he was just now seeing it. "I think you just had the blinders on from when we were kids. He was just so little and defenseless back then. You just seemed to miss him growing up. Either that or you really are blind."

I pretended my hands were scales and the blind side was the superheavy one. J practically shoved me off the couch, and I almost landed on my ass but managed to catch myself.

"Nerd. Now, I've got my own damn date to get ready for, so if you have any questions, you're just going to have to wait until we get back to work. I plan on spending the next three days without a phone, without ghosts, and preferably without people. Just some takeout and some Bishop—preferably sans clothes—but we'll probably have to work up to that."

J rolled his eyes at me, which was fair. After a six-year dry spell, Bishop would be lucky to escape with his life, let alone his clothes. Or I would completely chicken out. That was totally possible, too.

"Fine, you dork. I can't believe you're just coming back to work like you never left. You hear anything from the ABI?"

I snorted. Not only had I heard nothing from my mother or the ABI, neither had Bishop or Sarina. I'd asked—when shit finally calmed down enough to do so

—about it all, and all Bishop had said was that they were following procedure. Whatever the hell that meant.

"Nary a peep. I refuse to think bad things—at least for a little while. I'm going to enjoy the silence while I have it. Then it's back to homicides and bad guys."

I refused to believe the other shoe would always drop. Or at least I was trying really hard not to.

"Damn straight," J said, nodding like he couldn't wait to get back in the office with me. That was the rub about our job. None of us wanted there to be murders, but solving the riddles, working together? That was our happy place. Sorta.

I gave him a squeeze goodbye and booked it for my own house. I had T-minus twenty minutes until Bishop was supposed to arrive, and I hadn't packed, showered, or shaved my legs.

Letting myself into my front door, I looked around for the ghost of my grandfather before ripping off my top. I had zero time to dawdle. Hildy had been scarce these last few days, preferring to "keep an eye on things" elsewhere. I think he just didn't like seeing me and Bishop making out, but I couldn't be sure.

It was the tented white card with the loopy scrawl on it that made me freeze. No one should have been in my house. Other than Mariana, nobody with a pulse should have been able to break in—not without me knowing, anyway.

Hands shaking, I crossed the living room to the kitchen and reached for the paper. The cardstock was heavy, and I cursed myself almost instantly that I wasn't wearing gloves. Something told me it wouldn't matter, and I was proven right not a moment later.

Your mother can't protect you anymore, little one.

Game. On.

—X

This was what I got for thinking I could take a vacation.

Game on, brother.

Game. Fucking. On.

Darby's story will continue with

Dead Calm

Grave Talker Book Three

DEATH WATCH

Soul Reader Book Two

A prison break, a secret admirer, and a boatload of lies.

Just about everything Sloane Cabot knows about her past is a big old pile of malarkey. Couple that with the blank spot of how her family died, and she needs answers, like, yesterday.

But when a man shows up dead on her family's grave, she knows it somehow has to be tied to that fateful night a year ago.

Too bad you can't question the dead... *or can you?*

-Preorder now on Amazon-

Coming April 27, 2021

DEAD CALM

Grave Talker Book Three

There's not enough coffee or tacos in the world to deal with Darby Adler's family.

If it's not her death-dealing father, her back-from-the-dead mother, or her ghost grandfather, it's her long-lost siblings and their bid for power.

With ABI radio silent and her siblings to find, Darby's got a major problem on her hands. Especially when the local coven figures out that her father's no longer bound.

Can Haunted Peak, TN handle this family reunion?

-Preorder now on Amazon-
Coming June 29, 2021

THE ROGUE ETHEREAL SERIES

an adult urban fantasy series by Annie Anderson

THE PHOENIX RISING SERIES

an adult paranormal romance series by Annie Anderson

Heaven, Hell, and everything in between. Fall into the realm of Phoenixes and Wraiths who guard the gates of the beyond. That is, if they can survive that long…

Living forever isn't all it's cracked up to be.

Check out the Phoenix Rising Series today!

JOIN THE LEGION

EXCLUSIVE SNEAK PEEKS,
GIVEAWAYS, BOOK DISCUSSION.
COME FOR THE BOOKS.
STAY FOR THE MEMES.

To stay up to date on all things Annie Anderson, get exclusive access to ARCs and giveaways, and be a member of a fun, positive, drama-free space, join The Legion!

ABOUT THE AUTHOR

 Annie Anderson is the author of the international bestselling Rogue Ethereal series. A United States Air Force veteran, Annie pens fast-paced Urban Fantasy novels filled with strong, snarky heroines and a boatload of magic. When she takes a break from writing, she can be found binge-watching The Magicians, flirting with her husband, wrangling children, or bribing her cantankerous dogs to go on a walk.

To find out more about Annie and her books, visit
www.annieande.com

Made in the USA
Las Vegas, NV
14 November 2021